The Wanderer's Notebook Volume I

By Christopher Emrys

Cover Design & Artwork by Nicole Sato

Contents

The Wanderer's Notebook Volume I

I

The Sorrowful Sprite
Faetir, Year Unkept
Dynoltir, +1543 TR

The three sprites ran through what would appear to be a temperate rain forest after a hard rain. Wide, tall trees shaded the ground covered in bushes and ferns, moisture saturating every surface. The sprites raced after each other, climbing and leaping, sometimes in the trees, and sometimes near the ground.

Sprites possessed a strange combination of animal traits. They were typically small, only about 1 foot in length, with their tail being roughly half of that length. Their slender bodies were covered in something akin to glistening metallic scales, while patches of short fur bristled through the cracks. They had medium-length protruding snouts shaped like large reptiles, but their faces were more articulate, able to smile and snarl in a mammalian fashion. Long, pointed ears trailed behind their heads when they ran but were fully capable of twisting and turning as needed to locate sounds. A series of larger scales ran along their backs in two rows, one on either side of the spine. These plates could be raised in order to unfurl large, gossamer wings.

Though sprites could change shape and color at will, these three each had their own preference so that no matter what form they took, one tended to be blue, one red, and one green. On this particular day, Red was in the lead.

Red's mouth hung open in a subtle smile as she ran from her two playmates. The adrenaline surge at the prospect of being caught was exhilarating. She raced up a tree and out along one of its branches. Without hesitation, she leaped to the next branch and then ran down the far side of the trunk.

Almost as soon as she hit the ground, she heard Blue and Green land behind her. They must have used their wings to take a direct diagonal approach to the base of the tree.

Adrenaline shot through her again, and she raced ahead even faster.

Red dove straight into a large thick bush, ducking and leaping to avoid the branches. Her smile became less subtle as she caught sight of a peculiar scratch mark near the base of one of the branches. There was a slight depression in the soil below and after this particular branch. Red grabbed the branch with her front claws and swung herself over the depression. As soon as she'd passed it, she spun behind the base of the bush, flattened herself to the ground, and changed color to blend in.

She watched as Blue and Green tore along the ground a few seconds later. As soon as their feet touched the depression in the soil, the ground exploded as the two halves of a spiked trap slammed together, impaling her two pursuers in multiple places.

Red rolled over on her back laughing as her coloration returned to normal now that her concentration was broken. Blood poured from the wounds in the impaled blue and green sprites. She kicked her legs and pounded her fists into the ground as her body shook with laughter.

Blue and Green sagged in the trap. Their bodies went limp as the blood pooled on the ground.

Red's laughter was interrupted by the sound of the other sprites' bodies twisting and pulling away from the trap's center. They reconstituted themselves on either side of the trap and playfully pounced on her, their mouths hanging open in ear-to-ear grins.

The three sprites rolled around laughing and playfully biting at each other.

This was by far Red's favorite game. She and her friends had chased and trapped each other for as long as she could remember, and she never tired of it.

Eventually, their laughter died down. Red was getting sleepy and she knew they were as well. She curled up in a ball next to Green and Blue. The warmth of their bodies was comforting, and she sighed contentedly as she drifted off to sleep.

When the last of the three friends had fallen asleep, the forest around them began to fade, replaced by a white void. The only thing remaining were the three sprites curled up next to each other.

*　　　*　　　*

Green rubbed the sleep from her eyes and looked at her still sleeping friends. She was sure she'd heard something that had woken her up, yet the void around them was still empty.

Giving up on the sound, Green focused her mind on the area in front of her. The empty void faded into a lush patch of earth and vegetation. A bush grew out of the foliage and soon sprouted berries. Green went about eating her fill of the berries until she heard the sound again.

It was there but faint and unrecognizable. Her eyes squinted as she looked at her friends. What if they were producing the sound? A sly smile crept across her face as she mentally probed their minds, but, much to her disappointment, they were still asleep.

Green went back to eating the berries, looking around

for the sound's source. She found it captivating, as if it was beckoning her.

There.

The sound was coming from somewhere to her right. She slowly trotted off in the direction of the sound. Eventually, she came across a strange sphere of swirling colored lights. She'd never seen anything like it. The world was easy to mold with her mind, but this wasn't from her imagination. She reached back and mentally kicked her friends awake. Within seconds, they joined her and the three of them began chittering excitedly while curiously circling the sphere.

And then it came again, but this time louder, more distinct, and forming patterns she didn't recognize. She had no idea what the words meant, but there was a mental projection that went along with them. It was an invitation. They were being invited to enter the strange sphere. A new place to play was on the other side... new playmates and things to explore.

The offer was appealing, and she desperately wanted to go. Green turned and chittered to her two friends. They conferred for a few seconds.

The decision was unanimous. They all wanted to see this new land and what games they could play there.

Green leaped into the sphere.

*   *   *

Blue fell out of the swirling sphere of color and felt the soft, moist earth beneath his feet. He turned to look back and saw Red fall out behind him. Seeing that she landed safely, he turned and began taking in his new surroundings.

They were in a forest, though the plants were slightly different than the ones they normally conjured themselves.

4

The moisture in the ground and scents in the air indicated a recent rainfall. Red was clawing experimentally at a tree, and Green was digging into the earth near its roots. Blue's eyes followed the length of the tree upward and gazed on the clear blue sky between the leaves.

His thoughts were interrupted by confused chittering from Red. Blue turned his attention back to her and went to see what was going on.

Red continued to chitter away, poking at the tree and sending waves of mental images washing over him. The tree couldn't be changed. Blue, perplexed, tilted his head. What did she mean the tree couldn't be changed? Everything could be changed.

Blue flicked his mind at the tree to make it into a bush, but nothing happened. His head jerked lower and tilted again as he squinted at the tree. He focused harder, but nothing happened. In confusion, he clawed at the tree as if to dig through its surface and find the answers he sought, but nothing happened.

Waves of confusion washed out from him and over him from his two friends as they chittered away. Eventually the confusion faded and was replaced by a new thought: What sort of creature could and would overpower their will and keep the tree a tree? In their homeland, if two creatures were to vie for control of how the world was formed, it would normally be a matter of each participant changing things back to the way they were rather than completely denying or stopping the other from making the changes they desired.

The curiosity of it all took root in his mind and spread to the others. After a few moments of circling around and looking about, Blue and his two friends took off in the direction that instinct said they should go.

Green floated on her back in the cool waters of a stream they had found. Her arms and legs were relaxed and sprawled across the surface of the water. The sun shone brightly between the branches and warmed her hide, relaxing her muscles and her mind.

They had explored the forest for a few days but had not discovered anyone capable of reshaping the world or preventing them from doing so.

The three friends had, however, come across some of the local wildlife. There were small, soft, furry creatures with long ears who hopped away as soon as any of them approached. They had also encountered tall four-legged creatures with short fur, long pointed faces, and short tails. Some of these even had large, irregular, branchlike protrusions coming out of their heads, but, alas, even these creatures seemed unwilling to play.

They did have some luck with another creature with medium-length fur, a long tail, and four legs. It had sharper teeth and liked to howl at the sky for some strange reason. Every time it did, they could hear other howls, but they always seemed so far off. The three sprites followed the creature for a day, noticing that it kept trying to move closer to where the other howls had come from. Since it had sharper teeth and friends, they decided to see if it would be more open to playing than the other creatures they had encountered.

The three sprites circled the creature, nipping at it and running away to encourage it to chase them, but instead the creature responded with deep growls and bared teeth. It snapped at them a couple times, but they playfully dodged and laughed. Eventually, Blue managed to bite it back on its snout and draw blood. The sight of the blood was a sign that Blue had scored a point against their new playmate, but the creature ran off instead.

Disappointed, the three friends continued wandering aimlessly through the forest until they found a stream.

Green's eyelids became too heavy to keep open, and her mind drifted off.

Slowly Green became aware of a sound, different from what they'd heard in the forest so far, more fluid and continuous.

Green opened her eyes and turned her ears this way and that to isolate the direction whence the sound came. Once she honed in on it, she swam back to shore and crept along the bank until she spied its source.

The sound came from a tall, bipedal animal. Its flesh seemed mostly devoid of fur, except for an unusually long patch on the top of its head that flowed down around its shoulders. The head did not protrude in a snout-like fashion like so many other creatures, and its mouth seemed comparatively small. At first, Green thought that the upper torso was similar to hers with front legs ending in feet intended to grasp things...but its lower body was like a shapeless blob. After several minutes of observation, she realized that the shapeless blob extending up over the creature's torso and front legs was some other material and not the creature's own body. Green had never seen a creature that covered its body with some other material in this fashion.

The strange creature with the artificial secondary "skin" was checking a trap in the stream and pulling out several small, narrow, smoothly scaled and gilled creatures and depositing them in a wooden cylinder. Green easily recognized the trap for what it was. She and her friends made all sorts of traps for each other quite frequently.

Since this creature was the most like her that she'd seen

so far, Green began to look for a way to play.

The slippery scaly creatures looked tasty. Perhaps stealing one would make for a fun little game.

When the melodious creature turned its head away from the hollow wooden cylinder, Green snuck up and stole one of the slippery scaly things.

She scurried up a nearby tree and watched as the creature turned back to the cylinder and stopped its fluid sounds. The creature's head turned this way and that, looking for the missing thing. Green laughed so hard that she lost her grip on the scaly thing and it fell to the ground a few feet from the creature. Its head jerked up and its eyes locked on Green.

Green stopped laughing and stared back at the creature. It wasn't running away like the other creatures or making any moves to indicate that it wanted to play. The behavior was more like it was wondering what Green was.

Green tilted her head and made some cooing and clicking noises toward the creature. It picked up the scaly thing, placed it as far from itself as it could, and slowly backed away. Green tilted her head again as she looked at the offering. Did the creature want her to have it?

She carefully climbed down the tree and approached the scaly thing. If it was giving her the slippery little creature, she might as well eat it. Green took a few nibbles. Whatever this was, it was delicious.

The melodious creature slowly approached her and she stopped eating. She watched as it came closer and knelt down a couple feet away. The creature hesitantly reached out a hand. Green reached back and touched the soft flesh of the strange creature. Green's skin was tough and scaly, but this thing was very soft.

The creature made some sounds similar to its previous ones, but much less continuous, flowing, or pleasant. After a while, the creature stood to its full height and began walking away, taking its wooden cylinder with its tasty slippery, scaly things with it.

Green followed the creature back to what must be its home: a large wooden structure with square and rectangular openings.

*   *   *

By the time Red and Blue had followed Green back to the strange creature's large wooden box, night had fallen. Red split from her friends as they crawled and climbed all over the outside of the strange wooden box. There were two large, vertical rectangular sections that looked like they should open but didn't. Red also found a medium-sized square area that was divided in two vertically. It had a small ledge at the bottom. Red perched on the small ledge and nudged gently on the two panels. They moved slightly but would not open. She peered between the two panels and made out the faint silhouette of a horizontal piece that seemed to bridge the gap between the two panels on the other side.

Red extended one claw into the gap and shifted its shape so that it was longer and thinner, able to fit easily into the crack. She tried to lift the horizontal bar, but it would not budge. She gave up and rejoined her friends. Curling up with her two friends in a small hole under the edge of the wooden box, Red drifted off to sleep.

*   *   *

When morning came, Red was awakened by the sound of the large rectangular panel swinging open. The strange creature that Green had first met walked out of the wooden

9

box.

Red tapped her friends with her tail and they took off, circling and chittering around the strange creature. They poked at the material surrounding its lower half in curiosity. The strange creature made some sounds and another emerged from the box. The three sprites moved away a bit to get a better look.

This new creature was taller than the first and had fur on its face more than its head. The materials surrounding its body more closely followed the shape of its body and legs. It moved between the sprites and the first creature in a protective manner.

Red tilted her head and looked at the creature with the furry face. The other two laughed as her thoughts rolled over them. They scurried forward to poke at the new creature and it sprung forward, stamping its foot on the ground.

The sprites took off, only realizing that the creature was not following them when they were too far into the forest to still see the wooden box. They went back, but the two creatures were gone.

Red sat dejectedly on a branch and watched the wooden box, while the other two went off to explore the surroundings.

*   *   *

Green was getting bored of watching the strange creatures come and go from their wooden box. Over the last couple days, they had learned that a total of three creatures dwelt inside the box. They still didn't know what these things were, but over time they had come to realize that these three creatures were a family.

The original one they had found was apparently the

child of the group. It seemed to take commands from the other two creatures. They had followed it back and forth on its foraging trips into the forest. It would gather wriggling scaly animals from traps in the water, berries from bushes, or wooden cylinders filled with water and bring them back to the wooden box.

The second creature, the one with the furry face, was apparently an adult male. This one would travel a greater distance than the others and attach strange devices of wood and metal to a large, four-legged creature that walked on what seemed to be one large, dull, round claw on each foot. It had a long tuft of fur hanging over its backside and a streak of medium-length fur running down the back of its neck. This creature would then drag the strange device back and forth through a dull empty field, leaving deep grooves as it went.

Sometimes the adult male would wander even farther and kill other creatures before bringing them back to the wooden box. The larger ones would usually be skinned and carved up outside, but the smaller ones would be taken inside. Green and the others reasoned that the strange creatures must be eating these animals.

The last one they had learned of was the adult female. This one was somewhere between the size of the child and the adult male. It was very careful to make sure that the openings of the wooden box were always closed as soon as one of them entered or exited. This one also seemed the most distrusting of the three. Green had watched its body language, and while she thought that each of the creatures seemed protective of the others, this one seemed more... concerned. She didn't know what these creatures could be concerned about. In fact, such concern was such a foreign concept, that it had taken her quite a while to put her claw on it. What she observed in this creature was similar to what she'd experienced herself when she knew there was a trap but didn't want to step in it, and yet it was different. The creature's version was... more tense. It was almost as if the creature thought the trap's effects might be... permanent? Green shook her head. Permanent effects didn't make any sense. The world was malleable and so were they... or at least they should be.

Green snapped out of her reverie with a thought. Maybe it was time to introduce these creatures to a real game. This watching and waiting was getting boring. Perhaps an actual trap would liven things up.

Green scurried and leaped through the branches until she found Red and Blue. She relayed her idea, and her two friends agreed.

The next morning, Green waited by the side of the box for one of the creatures to exit. The large rectangle swung open, and the adult male stepped outside. Green chittered and ran up to it. She nipped at its leg and then ran off a bit and stopped. The adult male watched her. She took a few steps forward, then ran away a couple more feet. The creature took the hint and began to follow her.

After a couple more promptings, the creature's steps gained confidence and it quickly followed Green. She dashed around the corner of the wooden box. The adult male followed close behind. Its foot came down, pushing through the leaves and impaling it on several large, sharp thorns.

Green and the others began to laugh. The silly creature had walked into a trap. Soon it would return the favor and they would have endless fun!

After a moment, it occurred to Green that she hadn't heard it laughing. The sound had been much more... distressed? She turned and looked at the creature. Its face was not contorted into any semblance of fun that she'd seen before. It was something else.

Stranger still, she saw that the adult male's foot was still bleeding. Why wasn't it reconstituting itself? Why wasn't it having fun? None of this made any sense.

She tilted her head and looked at the creature. There was a new expression on its face. She wasn't sure what it was, but she got this strange feeling that it wasn't good. Something had changed inside the creature, but she wasn't sure what.

*   *   *

Blue dodged the long, flat, pointed piece of metal which the adult female swung at him via the object's wooden shaft. Ever since Blue figured out how to get into the strange creatures' large wooden box, they had been trying to hit him with wood and metal objects of various sizes. It was a lot of fun.

The sprite found the inside of the large wooden box to be fascinating. There were wood platforms of various sizes, shapes, and distances from the ground for him to climb on or hide beneath.

The strange bipedal creatures seemed much more enthusiastic about playing whenever Blue was inside their large wooden box.

Blue scurried around the box, over and under the various strange wooden and metal objects the creatures collected. The adult female would chase him all around the large, rectangular open space, but it could never catch him.

He jumped on top of a large wooden platform supported by four vertical wooden beams and turned to watch the adult female. He was on the far side of the rectangle, and the creature stopped. It moved to his right, so he moved to his left. It moved to his left, so he moved to his right. This game was exhilarating. He crouched low to the surface and snapped

13

playfully at the creature.

The creature began to move slowly to his left, so he moved right again. It continued in this direction until they had the narrower part of the rectangle between them. Blue crouched low, ready to spring at the first sign of attack. The creature slowly raised its wood and metal object. Blue dug his claws into the wooden surface.

The creature sprang forward, slamming the metal point into the space where Blue had been a moment before. The sprite's feet landed on the creature's head and he propelled himself upward and behind it, gliding through the air until he hit a rectangular wooden panel and dug his claws in for support.

Much to his surprise, the panel began to swing forward, revealing another large, open area inside the large wooden box that he had not seen before.

As the wooden panel swung fully into this new open space, Blue flew over and landed on a wide box in the middle of the space. The box, soft and squishy, gave way when he clawed at it curiously. As he touched it, it didn't move out of the way like mud did but held together more than moss. It didn't quite feel like fur or skin, which had the closest consistency that he could think of.

Blue was startled out of his reverie by a scream from the adult female as it came crashing through the opening to this new space and tried to attack him on the wide, soft box.

He successfully dodged its attack and leaped from the soft box to another box that was open on top and supported below by four wooden shafts. He gripped the side of the box tightly with his claws as he came to a sudden halt and looked down.

Inside the box was a small, pudgy version of these creatures. It was a little bigger than the sprite but didn't seem very agile. Laying on its back, it kicked its arms and legs weakly while smiling and laughing. It must be an even smaller child of these creatures.

Blue tilted his head as he looked at it. Well, if it could laugh, then maybe it could play.

The sound of something moving quickly through the air made him turn in time to see a long wooden shaft slam into his body and send him flying through one of the small openings in the large wooden box.

Blue hit the ground hard, knocking the wind out of him. The impact from the object left a lingering pain in his side, and the impact of the ground left another along his other side. These sensations not dissipating within seconds left him somewhat surprised and confused. As he rose to his feet, the pain made him wince and limp. He decided he didn't want to play for a while and carefully limped his way into the bushes so he could rest.

A few hours later, Blue still laid curled up in a hollow beneath a large root, wondering why the pain hadn't gone away. Normally, when they played games, the pain was temporary and any injury quickly mended itself. He poked at his side and winced as he felt one part of a rib move while the other stayed stationary.

He did not like this and the confusion and frustration it produced made him less inclined to play and more inclined to share his newfound sensations with the one who had introduced them to him.

*   *   *

Red could sense the desire to share pain emanating from Blue as he limped over to them. She tilted her head slightly and looked at him. This was a strange sentiment for

15

them. They liked to play, but they didn't want to inflict lingering or devastating pain the way Blue did now.

Her eyes caught the limp in his movements and she realized that he was still injured. This too was strange, as their injuries always healed within seconds.

Red chittered curiously at Blue, wondering why he hadn't healed yet. Blue had no answer. One of the strange creatures had hit him hard right after he had found a smaller, pudgier version in a wooden box.

In their homeland, healing usually required but the faintest of thoughts, while shapeshifting usually required more concentration. Red tilted her head again and wondered if Blue could shapeshift his body back into proper functioning. At this suggestion, Blue stopped. The thought hadn't occurred to him. The pain and frustration had consumed his mind, so he had forgotten that this was an option.

She watched as Blue closed his eyes and concentrated. She could hear his bones snap back into place and saw his expression relax as the pain subsided. Red chittered happily. She was pleased that her suggestion had eased his pain and cleared his mind. In moments, Blue was running and playing as if nothing had happened.

Red watched contentedly as Blue and Green ran around, chasing each other up and down trees.

*   *   *

Green and her two friends were perched along the rim of the wooden box that held the miniature version of the strange creatures. They had eventually shrugged off the strangeness surrounding Blue's inability to heal instantly and become distracted by his description of the miniature creature. Then they waited until the sun set and snuck into the large wooden box so they could all take a closer look. Gazing down at the creature, she wondered if it could play at all. Its body appeared softer and pudgier than the larger versions. If the bigger ones couldn't keep up, how could something even weaker?

Curiosity got the better of her, and she gently reached down to touch the sleeping miniature creature. As soon as she did, it opened its eyes and looked up at them with a strange expression. She leaned forward to get a better look, and the creature began making the most awful noise she had ever heard.

The auditory blight roused the other creatures from their slumber, and soon Green and her friends were dodging objects that were either being swung or thrown at them.

Green barely registered the increased passion in the larger creatures' attempts to catch them this time, as the joy of the chase flooded through her. It was exhilarating. These strange creatures were finally playing along at a pace that made the game truly exciting.

She and the others ran up and down the sides of the large wooden box, across or under every flat surface they could find as they were chased. The creatures were so intent on catching them this time that they were breaking things mere inches from where the sprites had just been.

Green ran toward the large movable panel and activated the latch so that it swung open as Blue jumped onto it.

She leaped to the ground, followed closely by Blue as they ran to the nearest tree and straight up its trunk. About halfway up, they ran onto a branch and turned to watch Red come dashing out of the box.

The adult male came rushing out of the box after Red with a long wooden shaft that ended in four metal prongs. Red was running up the side of the tree as the large creature threw the object at her, impaling her against the trunk.

Green and Blue took off.

*　　*　　*

A little while later, Blue and Green returned to where Red hung limply, impaled to the tree. They laughed and pointed at Red as she was the first of them to be truly caught by the strange creatures. She was the first to lose, and it amused them greatly.

After a while, it occurred to Blue that Red was not responding. Normally they would reconstitute themselves after a severe injury like this and the fun would continue. Why wasn't she moving? Why wasn't she pulling herself back together?

Memories of his own injuries earlier that would not heal instantaneously came upon him. A strange feeling washed through him that something similar might be happening to his friend. What if she couldn't even shapeshift herself back together?

Blue chittered at Green and they went over and began poking Red. She still didn't respond.

Perhaps the prongs were preventing her from reconstituting herself? Blue sent a mental image of his intention to Green and they worked together to pry the prongs out of the tree. The large object fell with a clatter and Red's body fell limply to the ground.

They scurried down and watched. Nothing happened. They poked Red's body again, but still nothing happened. They reached out as best as they could with their minds, but there was nothing.

The memories of the wounds that would not heal and

18

the trees that would not change at a thought flooded Blue's mind as he stared at Red's body. Was this how it was now? Was everything immutable? If Red's mind wouldn't even react, then how could she intentionally shift to fix her injuries?

Blue began to pace and circle frantically around Red's body. He was barely aware of Green sitting on the ground staring at Red with an almost blank look in her eyes. All of his attention was consumed by an ache in his chest, a tightness in his throat that felt like it was going spread to the space between his nose and his eyes, and a mass of confusion swirling in his mind.

This wasn't how the game worked. This wasn't how it was supposed to be. They were always able to reconstitute themselves and continue playing, yet the pattern of what they had already seen and the present reality before him was leading him to the inevitable conclusion that for Red, this end was final.

The tightness in his throat and sinuses increased. He could feel a frustration and emotional discomfort similar to when he was injured, but much worse. For the second time in his life, Blue did not want to play. He wanted to share his newfound emotional distress with those who caused it.

*   *   *

The next night, Green and Blue slipped silently into the large box. They quietly made their way around the box until they found one of the sharp metal objects that the strange creatures had tried to use against them in the past.

Green took the object and positioned herself next to the movable panel behind which the creatures hid. Once she was in place, she made some small sounds and Blue began to knock over objects on one of the flat, horizontal surfaces.

A few minutes later, the adult male poked its head out from behind the panel. Green watched as it slowly crept up on Blue, who was pretending not to notice.

As soon as the creature was out of the way, Green dashed into the next part of the box and up onto the big soft box. The adult female and the child were both still asleep on the large soft box. The adult female was closer. She carefully carried the sharp object over to the sleeping forms. When she was in position, she raised the object over the larger creature's throat and rammed it straight down into the soft flesh. Without pause, she pulled the object through the creature's throat and toward her, slicing as much of it as she could.

The creature began to make gurgling sounds and clutch at its throat. Green laughed at the futility of its efforts but was interrupted by the child waking and shrieking when it saw what was happening to the adult female. Green dashed forward with the sharp object and rammed it through the smaller creature's throat as well.

A sound caught her attention, and she turned as the adult male rushed back into this part of the box. Green dropped the object and dashed off of the large soft box as the adult male flung itself on its injured companions.

Green and Blue stood in the entrance to this section of the box and began laughing at the strange creatures. The adult male was clutching at the bleeding throats and wailing, but it was too late.

A strange sort of happiness washed over Green. There was a certain pleasure in knowing she was sharing with the adult male the sort of feelings she'd experienced, yet this pleasure did nothing to dissipate her own pain.

Eventually the child and the adult female stopped moving. The adult male collapsed on top of them as it produced strange noises that she could somehow tell were signs that the creature was experiencing emotions similar to what she had the previous night. Again, she felt a surge of satisfaction and pain.

Eventually, the creature became quiet. It got up, turned, and saw them. The creature's expression was different than any Green had seen it have previously. It picked up the pointy object and rushed at them.

They turned and ran for the movable panel to the outside world. Green jumped on the latch and Blue jumped on the wall like last time. As the panel swung open, there was a loud thud above her.

Green looked up to see Blue impaled to the panel by the pointy object. The ache in her chest and tightness in her throat returned instantly and she barely dodged the next object thrown at her.

Green fought to control the emotions as she dashed into the darkened forest.

*   *   *

After a couple days, Green returned to the creature's box. The pain and tightness had eased enough that she could concentrate on her new goal. Only the adult male remained. Once she caught it, then she would win.

She watched and waited until it was asleep before sneaking into the box. She placed a trip line in front of the panel to the outside world and gathered up all the pointy objects she could find. Green spent the next several hours planting the objects, pointy end up, in the ground in front of the movable panel. Then she made several trips up into the trees to gather leaves. She spread the leaves over the objects until they were well hidden.

Once she was done, she found the pronged object that

had impaled Red and wrapped a cord around it. Green took the other end of the cord and climbed up the box. She used it to pull the object up onto the top of the box. There she waited until morning.

*   *   *

As the sun rose, Green could hear sounds from within the box that could only be the adult male moving around.

Eventually, the sounds approached the movable panel, and Green prepared herself.

The creature opened the panel and tripped on the wire. It reached out to stop itself and impaled its hands and legs on the pointy objects. It screamed and tried to escape but impaled its hands and knees every time it tried to move, eventually losing balance and impaling its sides on more of the pointy objects when it fell again.

Eventually, the creature managed to roll out of the trap and lay on its back, breathing heavily and clutching at its wounds.

The creature looked up and saw Green.

She grabbed the pronged object near the prongs and jumped from the top of the box. Her weight brought the spikes straight down into the creature's midsection. It cried out in pain as Green jumped off and out of reach. She grabbed another pointed object and rushed back, impaling the creature's skull.

The creature went limp. Green slumped back to the ground.

She had won.

A sense of relief washed over her, and she relaxed as she lay back on the ground, staring at the sky. Her thoughts drifted to her friends, and the tightness and ache returned.

22

Green lay there, gazing into nowhere.

Sometime later, she was brought back to reality by a horrid sound. The image of the miniature creature sprang into her mind. She had completely forgotten about it.

She walked into the box and made her way to the miniature creature's small box. She climbed up the side and perched on the rim of the box.

Green looked down at the creature. This one was one of the creatures but also different from them. It had never played with them. It didn't take away her friends.

She tilted her head slightly. What was she to do with this thing? Should she keep it? Could it learn to play? Would it be a threat? Should she end it like the others?

The ache and desire to share her feelings returned as she looked at the creature that so closely resembled the ones who had taken her friends from her.

Possibilities and questions flowed through Green's mind as she sat and stared at the little creature.

II

Tabitha
Dynoltir, +2003 TR

Mina drifted awake as the car came to a stop. She blinked a few times, looking around the car and out the window to see where she was. The car had stopped in a driveway in front of a large, old house somewhere in the country. The house had two stories and no garage. The driveway formed a large arc that connected on both ends to the country road that she could see across the yard on the other side of the car.

She unbuckled her seat belt, opened the door, and climbed out of the car. The size and oldness of the house appeared foreboding, so she went and stood near her parents as they rummaged through the car's trunk. She felt more comfortable in their presence but couldn't take her eyes off the house, somehow not trusting it.

"Are you ready to see your new house and your new bedroom?" her mom asked as she took Mina's hand and led her toward the house.

Mina looked up at her mom; "Yes."

They walked up the steps of the front porch toward the door, and Mina looked around curiously. The porch was wide with a little fence around its border and wooden posts rising to the small ceiling that hung over it. The wood creaked slightly with every step.

Inside the house, directly across from the front door, a staircase led to the second floor on the left, and a long hallway on the right led to the back of the house. She could make out a door at the far end of the hall. Mina's mother took her to the first doorway on the right and showed her a large, empty room.

"This will be the dining room," her mother informed her before leading her down the hall to the next room on the right. The floors were wooden and creaked slightly as they walked down the hall.

The next room's purpose was clear to Mina as she looked around at the stove, sink, refrigerator, and cabinets everywhere.

They went back down the hall toward the front of the house and turned right, past the staircase and into another large empty room. This one had a doorway at the far end that led into another, slightly smaller room. Her mother explained that the first would be their living room where they'd watch TV and spend time with guests, while the second was going to be a room for her parents to do things in.

"OK, now for the bedrooms," her mother said as she led the way upstairs.

At the top of the stairs was a small landing that formed into a short hallway. There was a door on each end and one in the middle of the landing. Her mother explained that the middle one was for guests, and the one to the right was for her parents. They entered the room on the left.

Mina's new bedroom was shaped in a long rectangle that extended toward the front of the house to their left as they entered. To the left were a couple small windows evenly spaced along the wall. The wall straight ahead had one larger window in the center, and the back wall of the room had a doorway to a large closet.

"So, how do you like our new house?"

"It's very noisy," Mina replied.

"That's just because it's old. Old houses creak and make noises sometimes, but there's nothing to worry about," her mother reassured her. "Other than it being noisy, what do you think? Do you like it?"

"Yes! My bedroom is a lot bigger than in the apartment. I'll have much more room to play." Mina smiled as she walked around her room and explored her closet.

The next day, the moving truck arrived, and Mina's parents spent most of their time unpacking and setting up the house. Mina occupied herself by arranging her room and playing after her parents set up her bed between the two evenly spaced windows across from the closet.

Mina decided that she liked her new noisy home.

*   *   *

Mina drifted slowly into consciousness and opened her eyes. The darkness of her room was broken only by rays of moonlight that slipped between her curtains.

After a few moments, she decided she was thirsty and quietly slipped out of bed. Walking on the balls of her feet, she was able to move almost silently through her room to her door. She quietly opened the door and snuck onto the landing.

Now for the difficult part.

She carefully placed one foot on the first step close to the wall where it would creak less and slowly shifted her weight. With fingertips grazing the wall on one side and the railing on the other, she continued this process until she got to the bottom of the steps. Mina smiled when she reached the bottom without making a single creak. It had taken her half the summer to learn how to do that.

Keeping her left fingertips touching the rail, she turned in that direction and started her way down the hall, grazing the wall on her right with her other fingers. This was something else she'd learned to do on cloudy nights with no moonlight. It helped her know where she was even if she couldn't see that well in the darkness.

When she got to the kitchen, she turned on the light. The intensity blinded her, so she squinted until her eyes adjusted. Once she could see comfortably, she made her way to the sink. Her parents couldn't see the kitchen light from their room, making it safe to turn on. She filled a glass with water and began to drink it. Her mind wandered to the night time creaking of the old house. She realized she hadn't paid any attention to it for quite a while and wondered why she sometimes noticed things that were always there, yet sometimes she didn't.

As she finished her water, she noticed a difference in the creaking sound... more continuous, rhythmic... and moving down the hall toward the kitchen.

Mina turned with a start and stared at the doorway, expecting to see one of her parents at any moment.

She stared into the darkness as the creaking moved closer, until it stopped at the kitchen.

She looked but saw nothing.

"Mom?"

Silence.

"Dad?"

Silence.

Mina reached behind her and fumbled slightly as she placed the glass on the counter, never taking her eyes off the darkness.

She had to get back to her room, but she didn't want to go through where she had heard the sound.

Walking silently, she made her way to the doorway and looked both ways as quickly as possible.

Nothing was there.

Mina took one tentative step into the hall and heard a creak to her right. She shot off down the hall, grabbed the end of the rail, swung herself around, and ran up the stairs. She ran through her doorway, closed the door and launched herself under the bedcovers.

Mina peaked out of the covers, stared at her door, and listened.

Gradually sound settled in; she could hear the creaking move up the stairs until it stopped on the other side of her bedroom door.

Mina stared at the door, waiting for something to happen.

Only silence and stillness answered.

Mina continued watching until her eyes betrayed her, and her mind drifted off into oblivion.

*   *   *

Peace and emptiness surrounded Mina. Slowly she became aware of a slow, rhythmic sound. It ebbed and flowed like a wave moving near then far, over and over.

Curious, her mind began focusing on the sound. As she did, she noticed that it was made of smaller sounds. Each one became slightly louder, slightly closer, until she felt she could almost touch it.

Then, the sounds would move away, growing quieter.

Somehow the little sounds seemed familiar and irregular, never quite the same.

Creaking, creaking, like the wooden floors in her house.

Mina's eyes shot open to stare into the darkness over her bed. It was just a dream. That was all. She'd only been dreaming about the strange noises from the other night.

The creaking moved away from her doorway again. Mina turned, pulled the covers over her, and peaked through a crack between the blanket and the bed as she watched her door.

Slowly, the creaking steps reached their farthest point near her parents' bedroom door, before slowly coming closer and closer again. Mina stared silently at her door, hoping it was one of her parents, but the steps came to a halt and nothing happened.

Something scraped down the outside of her door. Mina hid under the covers. The sound stopped and she waited.

She carefully peaked out again at the still closed door.

Something scraped down the outside of the door, the handle turned, and the door flung open.

Mina screamed into the darkness.

Within moments, her parents had rushed into her room, turning on the lights as they went in.

"What's wrong?" her mother asked, sitting down beside her and hugging her.

"Someone was walking back and forth outside my room, and then they started clawing at the door. The door swung open, and I screamed."

Her mom looked worriedly at her dad, but he was already heading back out of her room. "I'll check the house, you stay with her," he said.

Mina could see him check the guest room before heading downstairs.

She clung to her mother as they waited. After a while, her dad returned and sat down on her other side. "Everything is locked and no one else is in the house," he said as he put his arm around her.

"It was probably just a bad dream. Would you like to sleep with us tonight?" her mother asked.

Mina wasn't convinced, but she nodded, and her parents led her across the landing to their room.

*   *   *

Sunlight flooded the kitchen as Mina ate breakfast with her parents.

"Are you looking forward to starting school next week?" her mother asked.

Mina paused for a moment to consider; "Yes and no."

"Why not?"

"Well, I won't be able to sleep in the middle of the day as much."

"Why don't you sleep at night?" her father asked, his fork paused halfway between his plate and mouth.

"The footsteps still keep me up, but I'm getting used to it," she replied and continued eating. She barely noticed her parents glance at each other.

*   *   *

Mina lay in bed, the rhythmic creaking steps almost lulling her to sleep, until she heard her door open.

Her mind jumped back to consciousness as her head snapped down and to the side to stare at her doorway.

Darkness and silence loomed within the borders of the door frame, but she couldn't see the whole landing from this angle. Mina pulled the covers over her head and stared, waiting.

Several long moments passed before the creaking footsteps resumed, but this time they were closer. The sounds approached her head, then moved away down the length of her bed before turning and rounding the foot. Then they slowly moved closer to her again. Her hairs raised on the back of her neck. She wanted to look but was too afraid to move.

30

After a pause, the footsteps began retracing their path. Mina strained her eyes to see as the footsteps neared the head of her bed and paused by her head. There was nothing.

The floor creaked as the steps made their way back toward the foot of her bed.

"Just go away," whispered Mina, and a cold hand grabbed her foot.

Mina screamed and moments later her parents rushed into her room. She threw herself at her mother with tears streaming down her face.

"Something grabbed my foot."

She heard her father walk out of the room as her mother embraced her; "You're OK, you're OK."

Her father returned a short while later. "It was probably just another bad dream."

Mina pushed herself away from her mother and looked at her father, "No! It was real. I wasn't even asleep."

She watched her parents exchange looks and knew they didn't believe her.

Her mother hugged her again, "I'll stay with you tonight so you can sleep. You want to be well rested for school tomorrow."

Her father gave her a hug. "Sleep well," he said before returning to his room.

Mina lay in her mother's arms for a while thinking about what had happened. She was too angry that they didn't believe her to fall asleep immediately, but eventually fatigue won.

*   *   *

Mina sat alone at one end of the long lunch table in the cafeteria of her new school. She poked at her food but wasn't really hungry. It was her first day, and she was exhausted.

She rested head in one hand and stared blankly at her tray. Her mind began to fade and her eyelids fluttered.

"Are you OK?" said a strange voice.

Mina straightened up and looked in front of her. One of the girls from her class sat on the other side of the table. She vaguely remembered seeing the girl sitting in the back corner of the classroom when she first got there. The girl had energetic eyes, a kind smile, and slightly unkempt hair. The combination of the smile and the frizzled, unkempt hair added a sort of friendly craziness to her appearance.

Mina stared blankly at the girl, not knowing what to say.

The girl tilted her head to one side. "Why are you so tired?"

"You wouldn't understand."

"I would if you told me," she said with a smile.

Mina was silent.

"Why haven't you slept? Is everything OK?"

"My house is haunted," whispered Mina. She looked at the other girl's expression, waiting for her to laugh or dismiss her. Instead, the girl got a strange smile on her face.

The other girl leaned forward and scrunched up her nose, smiled mischievously, and whispered, "My daddy says we eat the monsters!"

Mina smiled and the other girl laughed.

"I'm Mina."

"My name is Tabitha. I would love see an actual ghost. Do you think I could come over to play sometime?"

"I don't know; I'd have to ask my parents."

*   *   *

32

The morning light streamed through the kitchen curtains as Mina joined her parents for breakfast. She felt energetic this morning, and it took her awhile to realize that she'd fallen asleep to a quiet room the previous night for the first time in weeks.

"How was your first day of school?" her father asked.

"I made a new friend. Her name is Tabitha," she replied.

"I'm so glad to hear that," her mother smiled at her.

"Can Tabitha come over and play after school?" Mina asked.

"We would need to talk to her parents first to make sure it's OK," said her father.

"If you can get her phone number, we can call them tonight," offered her mother.

"OK," Mina said, smiling as she went back to eating.

After a minute, her mother got up from the table and left the room.

Her mother walked back into the kitchen, and addressed her father, "Have you seen the car keys?"

"Aren't they on the hook by the front door?"

"No, I can't find them anywhere."

"Mina, have you seen the keys?"

"Nope," she replied through mouthfuls of cereal.

Her parents started searching the house, becoming more agitated as time passed.

"Mina, help us look." She could hear the stress in her mother's voice.

"OK." Mina got up and started looking around the living room. It was odd for her parents to misplace their keys. She'd rarely had to help them look for the keys in the past.

After several minutes, her mother yelled her name from upstairs. Mina ran up to her room and found her mom standing in front of her closet.

"Why were my keys in your closet?"

"I don't know."

"Did you hide them? Was this supposed to be a joke? Were you playing with them?" her mom asked angrily.

"I wasn't playing with your keys," Mina replied with irritation at the false accusation.

"Don't talk to your mother with that tone."

"You shouldn't lie to us," said her mother.

"I'm not lying," screamed Mina as she stormed out of the room.

*   *   *

Mina turned the light off in her room and crawled into bed. Her room was peaceful and quiet with rays of moonlight sneaking in between her curtains. She lay in bed staring mindlessly at the silver patterns they painted on her walls. Her consciousness began to drift away and her eyes closed slowly.

Then the creaking steps began.

Mina came back to wakefulness instantaneously and tried to look through her doorway into the darkness of the landing. The steps moved steadily nearer until they passed through her doorway and began circling her bed again. This time she could feel something pressing into her mattress as the steps passed.

Mina lay still in the center of her bed, her eyes following the invisible path of the steps.

The creaking footsteps made their way back to the side of her bed nearest the door and paused. Mina couldn't see anything, but she had the distinct feeling of something leaning in close to look at her. She pulled herself away and further into her blanket as she stared into the darkness.

The steps moved away, back onto the landing. Mina relaxed slightly. Perhaps it was leaving. Maybe now she could get some sleep.

The creaking stopped at the far end of the landing. Several long moments passed in silence, and Mina began to close her eyes.

Then the footsteps ran across the landing, through her room, and something heavy landed hard on her bed.

Mina screamed.

A few moments later her father walked in. "You need to be quiet. You have school tomorrow, and your mother and I have work in the morning."

"But something hit my bed."

"We heard you laughing on the landing then run to your room and scream," he said with irritation in his voice. "Just go to sleep."

Mina was confused and angry. She hadn't been playing on the landing, and her father shouldn't be accusing her of something she didn't do.

"It's not me!"

"Stop lying to us. There's no one else in your room. You need to grow up," he said in irritation before leaving her room and shutting the door.

Mina sank into her blankets, alone in the darkness.

*   *   *

The doorbell rang as Mina and her parents were finishing supper in the dining room. She watched her father leave the room to answer the door. Mina and her mother heard a few muffled words before he returned.

"We have a guest tonight," he said as he walked back into the room.

Mina turned to see who it was and was surprised to see Tabitha standing in the doorway.

"Mina, did you invite a friend over without telling us?" her mother asked, giving her a hard glare.

"No. Tabitha suggested it, but I didn't tell her she could come over."

"Your father took off pretty quickly. I didn't even see taillights driving away when I opened the door," her father commented to Tabitha.

"Don't be upset at Mina. I invited myself," Tabitha said with a smile.

Her parents exchanged glances, and her mother turned to address Tabitha.

"Don't worry, Mrs. Parker, I'll make sure Mina stays quiet tonight. My dad will pick me up in the morning," Tabitha offered before turning to Mina. "Come on, let's go up to your room."

Mina's mother closed her mouth in astonishment. She nodded to Mina, and the two girls left the room.

*   *   *

The girls sat quietly on the bed in Mina's dark room. Her parents had gone to bed several hours ago, and all was silent and still in the house.

Tabitha yawned. "I'm getting sleepy. The ghost isn't here, so we might as well go to sleep. I really wanted to see a ghost though."

Mina looked at her friend. It was hard to tell if she was just disappointed or if she didn't believe that the ghost was real.

"I'm going to go get a drink of water before I go to sleep. I'll be right back," Tabitha said before walking out of the room.

Mina pulled her knees up to her chest and wrapped her arms around her legs. Her parents were mad at her again, and her one friend probably thought she was a liar. She didn't know what to do as she became acutely aware that she was the only thing in the expanse of empty darkness all around her. Staring mindlessly at the silver lines of moonlight on her floor, she wasn't sure why she should bother caring anymore.

A slight creak came from across the room. It was followed a moment later by another. The steps gathered speed as they approached her bed.

Mina's blanket was ripped off the bed and thrown across the room as a great weight slammed into the mattress in front of her. A cold hand gripped her ankle and began to pull her to the foot of the bed. Mina screamed as she was forcefully dragged across the bed and thrown to the floor in the middle of the room.

Her parents staggered into the bedroom, angry and sleep deprived. They turned on the lights. "Stop making so much noi—"

The light bulb shattered, and the room was plunged into darkness again.

Mina could see nothing as her eyes tried to adjust back to the darkness. Her parents' sounds of frustration quickly changed to fear as an angry growl filled the room. She heard the sound of two large objects hitting a wall. She turned her head and could barely make out the forms of her parents lying on the floor on the other side of the bed.

Mina began to scramble backward as she saw two red dots appear in the darkness above her parents. The red dots moved toward her and as they passed through a moonlight beam coming through the blinds, she got a brief glimpse of a ghastly pale visage, withered and twisted with hate.

The red eyes stopped inches from her face, and she felt cold hands grip her tightly and lift her off the ground. There was no one left. Her parents were unconscious and she was alone, held aloft by an angry ghost. There was nothing she could do. Tears rolled down her face, and this time she felt cold, frozen air pass over her as the thing growled again.

Mina looked away. And that's when she saw the figure in the doorway. It was Tabitha. She was just standing there.

"Run!" she screamed at her friend, but Tabitha didn't move.

The growl stopped and the red eyes turned toward the door.

"My daddy says we eat the monsters," came the reply, as a wicked smile spread across Tabitha's face and the darkness of the night around her grew darker still. The shadows coalesced until all that was left was a Tabitha-shaped void.

The ghost dropped Mina, and she saw its eyes move farther from the doorway where Tabitha stood. Tendrils of shadow reached out from the void and wrapped themselves around the unseen form of the ghost. Mina reached up to cover her ears as it shrieked in an unholy agony.

In the moonlight, she could see the faint outline of the thing claw at the floor as the shadowy tendrils dragged it inexorably closer to the void. Wood splintered and cracked and the walls shook with the ghost's terrified shrieks.

Mina watched in horrified fascination as the ghost was dragged into the void and consumed.

The shadows around Tabitha subsided slowly, and the void became her classmate again.

Mina backed away when Tabitha approached her.

"It's OK. I'm not going to hurt you. I'm your friend."

"But..."

"It's OK," reassured Tabitha as she knelt before Mina. She reached out and gently stroked Mina's hair. Strangely, she felt herself begin to relax.

"You can rest now. Let the darkness of night fulfill its true purpose, giving you rest and peace."

That was the last she heard as her exhausted mind relaxed into a restful sleep.

III

Aurelia
Dynoltir, +153 TR

Aurelia made her way through the market, enjoying the sunlight on her skin as she frolicked from one stand to another. She was barely aware of her bodyguard, a soldier under her father's command, as he kept pace behind her. Each new stall she visited had some unique item or beautiful new cloth.

The buildings around the market were mostly square structures made of clay and brick that shared walls. The market stalls themselves tended to be wooden constructs with fabric awnings that could be set up and closed down each day.

Aurelia's guard wore the plated armor of the Reman Empire that covered mostly his torso and shoulders. Aurelia herself was always dressed in the latest fashions. Her jet-black hair fell just past her shoulders, and her eyes were open and bright.

"Aurelia, it is so good to see you."

Aurelia turned to see Cassandra approaching her from the next stall over. They greeted each other with an enthusiastic hug. Aurelia noted the location of her friend's armed escort a few feet away.

"Have you seen this new fabric that just came in?"

"I know, it's amazing. Imagine what a beautiful dress could be made out of it."

They chatted excitedly as they made their way down the street, each followed by their own escort.

"Miss, it is nearly time for your lessons. Your father charged me to make sure you made it to them this time," interrupted Aurelia's guard.

40

Her shoulders slumped and she frowned at the guard. "Father just wants to ruin everything." She paused, tilted her head, and looked at the guard with a flirtatious smile. "You know, you don't have to do everything Father tells you to."

The guard stared at her with a stoic expression. "I must insist. I have my orders."

Aurelia slumped again and turned to her friend. "I'm so sorry, Cassandra. I'm afraid I must be going."

"It's OK. I'm sure we'll see each other again soon. My parents are planning a banquet a week from now. We can catch up then if I don't see you sooner."

"Oh yes, definitely. I cannot wait." Aurelia leaned in and whispered, "Will your cousin be there? He's so handsome in his captain's uniform."

Cassandra playfully slapped her on the shoulder; "Gross, he's my cousin!"

Aurelia's guard cleared his throat and interrupted again, "We must be leaving."

"Fine, fine," said Aurelia, rolling her eyes. She hugged her friend goodbye, gave the guard a dirty glare, and made her way down the street.

*   *   *

"Stand outside like a good little wet blanket, will you," said Aurelia as she turned from the guard and entered the dwelling of Koios, her tutor.

"Aurelia, my dear. It's so good to see you," the older man said as he ushered her into the back room where they conducted her studies. Koios was older than Aurelia's father, with much more gray seeping into his hair. His face was lined with age, his eyes bright, and a smile always at the corner of his lips.

41

"And you as well, Tutor," Aurelia said as they closed the door to the back room.

"It's good to finally be around an intelligent person," Aurelia quipped as all frivolities dropped from her demeanor. Her eyes hardened, her smile disappeared, and her stride became direct and purposeful.

"You know, you don't need to pretend all the time. Would it really be so horrible if the rest of the world knew you as I do: an intelligent and capable young woman?"

Aurelia made her way to the work bench and began examining the newest partially dissected specimen. "Their ignorance is my strength. If they think me as vacuous as the rest of them, then they will never perceive me as a threat. This is to my advantage." She opened a scroll and compared the sketches she'd made previously to the specimen on the table before her.

"We've dissected these before. Don't you have anything new?"

"I do, actually, even if you're changing the subject. Come, it's in the basement."

Koios frequently visited the local docks to acquire new and exotic life forms to examine. He had developed a relationship with the local traders and sailors so that now they would save anything unusual just for him.

"Some traders from the north caught this creature a few weeks back. They said it was mostly starved and quite vicious when they first found it. That's why they fitted it with the spiked shackles. Unless the creature was being injured by the attempt, it would not cease trying to break free and attack them."

They entered a narrow stairway, which led down to a lower level that Koios frequently used for storage and experimentation. Since the house was on the edge of the city near a jagged rocky slope leading down to the sea, the first room of the lower level led to another that opened up facing the slope and the sea. It provided fresh air and an easy way to dispose of dissected animal corpses. Keeping specimens in the lower level also allowed him to more freely study in a space that casual guests would not normally see.

The traders had brought the creature down into this first room and chained it inside a cage he kept for live specimens. "What is it?" asked Aurelia as she approached the cage to get a better look, her back straight and hands clasped behind her.

The creature was exceptionally pale, male, and roughly humanoid. If not for slight movements, she should have thought it to be dead. Its ears were slightly pointed, its body was emaciated, and its fingernails were slightly more claw-like than normal human nails. If it stood up instead of crouching, and was an actual man, it would probably be considered a tall one.

"I don't know. Neither did the traders. It speaks in some barbarian tongue that even the traders had never encountered. They also said it reacts quite violently to sunlight, which seems to cause it excruciating pain."

"Fascinating," muttered Aurelia as she retrieved a mirror from a nearby table. She placed it in a beam of sunlight and tilted it. The beam reflected off the mirror and hit the creature full in the face. It shrieked, closed its eyes, and tried futilely to move out of the light. It was then that Aurelia realized the creature was not just caged, it was chained. She chided herself momentarily for her lack of observation as Koios's previous statement about spiked shackles came to mind. The bands of metal around its wrists, ankles, and neck all had spikes protruding inward that were caked with old blood. The creature's flesh was raw and barely healed where it must have frequently cut itself on the spikes.

Disgust grew in her heart as she gazed on a creature so undisciplined and foolish as to cause itself such injury from its own rage.

*   *   *

Wyrm sat in the shadows of the cage listening to the strange babbling of the people who held him captive. He'd been so starved in the few weeks previous that he'd attacked some traders as they camped near the river. His hunger had made him weak, and he'd been subdued easily. They had kept him locked up below deck until they arrived at this sun-cursed land. At least his homeland in the mountains had been cloudy enough to lessen the painful rays of the sun.

The voices grew louder as the old man and a young woman came down the steps. He had no idea what they were saying to each other, but the woman stared at him for a while before she found a mirror and bent the sunlight directly onto him. He instinctively cried in pain and tried to get away, but the chains prevented him from moving more than about half a foot in any direction.

He glared at her angrily even after she removed the beam of light from his face. He could smell the singed hairs on his body, and his eyes still burned.

The two humans babbled on a few minutes more, and then the woman did it again, this time aiming the beam at his torso. Wyrm writhed in pain. Why was she doing this? She tilted the beam away from him.

His anger began to build. This was worse than before. He'd spent his whole life being treated like scum, tossed around and beaten whenever the urge struck someone. She was like Them. Wyrm closed his eyes, trying to will the pain

44

away.

The woman angled the beam on him again. He hated her. She needed to die.

Wyrm turned and glared at her through the pain of the burning light. It didn't matter anymore how much it hurt. He was going to kill her. He'd put up with being treated like this long enough. Wyrm strained against his chains, his lips curling in a growl to reveal his sharp, pointed teeth as they ground together. The spikes dug into his flesh, but he didn't care anymore. Bitterness and anger made the pain moot. If his pain would lead to the suffering of this vile creature that kept tormenting him for her own amusement, then it was worth it. Any pain she felt would more than outweigh his own suffering.

The woman and the old man were beginning to back away from his cage. Wyrm pushed harder and harder, his rage helping him ignore the agony as the spikes tore through his skin and into his muscle and tendons. He could feel the blood flowing over the wounds, but he didn't care. The death of his tormentor was all that mattered. Nothing else mattered; he could almost feel the chains about to break. Hatred filled his eyes.

And then his eyes began to dim. The blood loss didn't even register to his mind, but it registered to his body. Wyrm collapsed.

*   *   *

The creature's angry outbursts died down slowly as its physical damage drained it of the energy needed to fuel such emotions.

"It would be wise to avoid unnecessarily antagonizing a creature so willing to do itself damage in order to attack you," Koios admonished.

"Experimentation and observation are key to learning and understanding everything in the natural world," returned Aurelia. "Besides, the chains appeared to be of sufficient quality to hold the creature, and, in the event that they failed, the cage itself would have stopped the creature or delayed it long enough for us to get outside where sunlight would have protected us. You can see clearly that the flesh is burned where the reflected sunlight touched its skin." Aurelia turned her back on the creature as she replaced the mirror. "If all else failed, the guard could have killed it. Multiple contingencies were in place. There was no need to worry."

Koios shook his head, half smiling at her cunning, but slightly disappointed and worried about her coldness.

"We should learn what this creature eats so that our subject does not die on us prematurely," he offered.

"Not—" Aurelia started.

"Not more than necessary so that it does not gain enough strength to escape. Yes, I am well aware of that," continued Koios.

He led her back up the stairs and into a side room where he began to prepare several small bowls with bits of different foods while Aurelia recited her latest reading assignments as well as her analyses of the topics they'd discussed at her last visit.

Koios prepared six small bowls, each with its own sampling of one of six possibilities: meat, vegetables, or fruit divided into cooked and raw variations. They returned to the lower level and quietly placed the tray of bowls next to the cage before retreating to a safe distance.

Koios retrieved a couple stools, and they sat and waited, quietly discussing the day's lessons.

After some time, the creature began to stir. Koios

watched it closely, also glancing at Aurelia every so often to observe her reactions to it. As usual, her face was impassive, betraying little of her mind's inner workings. He returned to observing the creature.

The creature sat up slowly and looked at them. Its eyes hardened into hate as soon as it shifted its gaze from Koios to Aurelia. Koios saw no change to her expression in response.

Koios gestured to the food, and it finally began to examine the bowls in front of it. The creature looked at each bowl in turn until it came to the bowl of raw meat. Tentatively, it reached out its semi-clawed hand and picked up the raw meat. Instead of taking a bite like Koios expected, the creature licked the meat. It then sank its teeth into the meat and seemed to be sucking on it. Koios looked to see Aurelia raise an eyebrow when the creature finished sucking on all parts of the meat and began to lick up the small amount of blood in the bowl.

"It feeds on blood," she whispered. "Fascinating."

Koios turned back to the creature. He looked closely at its emaciated form. The hair was long and unkempt, the skin sickly pale, and the nails almost claw-like. He wasn't sure, but it almost looked like the edges of the burns from the reflected sunlight were beginning to heal even as he watched. He made a mental note to observe carefully any changes in the creature's condition when it consumed blood so that he would not feed it enough for it to become an insurmountable threat.

*   *   *

Aurelia and her father parted ways as she was led to the hall where Cassandra and the other women were holding their half of the banquet. The large rectangular room was supported by an inner rectangle of pillars. The tables were low to the ground, and everyone reclined on cushions while eating.

Aurelia greeted her friend and several of the other women before taking her place at the table. Her eyes were wide and bright, a smile or appropriately sympathetic expression always on her face whenever she spoke with anyone. Most of the conversations detailed the latest fashions, exotic imports, popular playwrights, or captivating gladiators. Aurelia engaged in these topics with bright enthusiasm, only feigning ignorance when the topics shifted to more serious matters.

"Have you seen that new gladiator Cassandra's father bought?"

"He's so handsome."

"They say he's from Elissana."

"I think they just make those stories up."

"I'm surprised that Cassandra's cousin hasn't been shipped off to fight against Elissana yet."

"Well, actually, he's going to be leading a legion and leaves in three months," replied Cassandra.

"He's going where? What's Elissana?" asked Aurelia, a look of confusion and worry crossing her face.

"My child, for a general's daughter, you certainly know very little," interjected an older woman with a look of disdain from the other side of the table.

Aurelia hung her head slightly. "I'm sorry, the things he talks about are just so boring; it's hard to remember."

The woman laughed.

Eager to improve the tone, Cassandra continued, "When he returns victorious, he will be promoted and eligible to join the Council."

Another woman scoffed. "Your father is spending a lot money supplying an army and risking his nephew to gain another ally on the Council."

"It won't do much good; Marcus and Castor each control too much of the Council for Cassandra's father to ever be elected to the Imperial Senate."

"I heard that they have a deal where their allies alternate voting between them every cycle, so they take turns representing the region in the capital."

"I heard that the whole thing almost fell through when one of Marcus's allies discovered that his daughter was the mistress of one of Castor's allies a few years back."

"They almost came to blows in the council hall."

"It was a huge scandal."

Aurelia listened closely as the night wore on, displaying more interest when topics veered toward the superficial, but feigning just enough ignorance on serious or political matters to illicit explanations and encourage more discussion from those around her.

Eventually, the feast ended, and Aurelia and her father returned home to their estate.

*   *   *

Wyrm warily watched the old man place the bowl of blood in front of the cage. As soon as he'd backed off, Wyrm leaped at the bars and grabbed the bowl. He ravenously consumed the red liquid, then lay back against the wall. His eyes closed as he felt his pains ease.

A soft scratching sound caught Wyrm's attention and he opened his eyes. The old man was sitting on a stool behind a small table in front of the cage looking intently at him then down at a parchment on which his stylus scratched. It took Wyrm several long moments before he realized the old man was drawing him.

Wyrm leaned forward, gestured at his eyes, then at the

parchment. The old man lifted it so he could see. The images were a set of variations focused on his neck, with the first showing severe wounds, and the rest showing the gradual healing of said wounds. There were markings of some sort near the diagrams, but Wyrm didn't know what they were.

He touched his own neck and realized that there was no pain, and his fingers could not detect a scar. They had been giving him small amounts of blood for the past several days, and he had noticed that he'd started feeling better, but it hadn't occurred to him that less pain meant the wounds had closed.

Wyrm began to look at himself and noticed that his body did not seem so emaciated as before. He stood up and began stretching and flexing his body. He actually felt really good.

His thoughts were interrupted by the old man getting up and going back upstairs. After some time, he returned with the young woman. Wyrm glared at her as she entered the room, though his anger toward her was not as great as it once was. He did not like the way she treated him. He'd stopped wildly trying to kill her every time she entered the room several days previous when the chains had torn his body so badly that he'd passed out and awakened to find that he couldn't clench his fists any longer. He clenched them now, released, and sat down.

He could wait.

Wyrm stared mindlessly into the distance until the slightly more agitated actions of the old man caught his attention. He stared intently at them as they continued speaking in their strange language. The old man did not seem happy about something, but the young woman showed no expression as she gestured toward Wyrm.

An image of a knife cutting into his hand flashed through his mind.

His two captors continued their discussion for a few seconds more before the young woman reached for a knife on the table. The old man put his hand over hers, stopping her from picking it up.

The young woman relinquished the knife and returned upstairs, followed shortly afterward by the old man.

*   *   *

The full moon's rays peaked over the roofs of the buildings just enough to allow Aurelia and Cassandra to make their way. Aurelia kept the hood of her cloak pulled close over her face to ensure no one would accidentally recognize her as she followed her friend. Cassandra would look back from time to time with an excited smile or stifled giggle, and Aurelia would return one in kind.

Eventually they reached a door at a dead end in a narrow side street and put on their masks. The masks were plain wood carved to resemble nondescript human features. Cassandra knocked on the door, and a small window was opened. Aurelia could make out a pair of eyes peeking through as Cassandra raised her palm toward the door, revealing the symbol hidden on the underside of a silver ring.

The window was slammed shut, the door was opened, and the two entered.

A servant with a lantern led them down a flight of steps and around a corner into a large, open, dimly lit room whose roof was supported by an inner ring of pillars. The room was crowded, so Aurelia and Cassandra held hands so as to not lose each other. They maneuvered their way to the right side of the room, still near the back.

Aurelia scanned the crowd. Many wore cloaks, but some wore their normal attire, undisguised. Judging by the

51

materials, colors, and designs, most of the attendees were likely to be the offspring of the city's wealthier families. Every now and then, she spied rougher, more callused hands, meaning that there were servants or soldiers in attendance as well.

These back-alley cults were known to crop up from time to time, catering to thrill-seeking youths eager to rebel against the more established temples and deities. Aurelia kept her free hand on the dagger that she had hidden in the folds of her dress. These cults were also sometimes the cause of the injury, death, or disappearance of the city's wealthy youth.

Despite the risk, Aurelia was interested in the opportunity such an organization presented. It gave access and influence to wealthy families while maintaining anonymity. Rising through the ranks of such a secretive cult was much less conspicuous than attempting such through one of the more established temples.

The priest entered from a doorway at the far end, near the altar, and the rituals began.

*   *   *

"Why do you cut open the animals?" Wyrm asked Koios as he watched the old man cut open and examine another strange sea creature. Once he was well fed and healed, pain and hunger no longer consumed his mind. Over time, he had learned his captors' language but had little reason to speak with them. He was still caged like an animal, after all. While they might seem nice, they were hardly trustworthy. He had watched them discuss a strange array of topics, many of which did not seem immediately useful or important. They would even cut open various animals, but never eat them. Eventually, the strangeness of it all got the better of him.

Koios looked over at him and replied, "I dissect the specimens in order to learn more about them. Since the animals are usually brought to me by fishermen, I am unable to observe their behaviors, but I can observe how they are composed internally."

"Why do you care? If it's not food or clothes, what use is it?"

Wyrm watched Koios set down his knife and turn to face him more fully. "We observe the world in various ways and ponder our observations so that we can better understand how the universe works."

"The world works by the strong preying on the weak. If we're hungry, we eat. If we're tired, we sleep. Why should we care about some fish we've never seen? What's the point?"

"Curiosity is usually a driving factor, but observation and meditation can lead us to new ideas and understandings. It's true that they sometimes are not immediately useful, but the key is to learn how a principle in one thing can be applied to another. Through my many dissections, I have learned that there are similarities between the organs of many animals. Different types of fish are more similar to each other than to different types of birds. Animals like dogs and horses fall into another category as well. With my prior work on the battlefield, I have seen the insides of humans. From observing the patterns in all of these creatures, I can look at you and estimate where your heart is, how to kill you, and how to stitch you back together."

Wyrm stepped back slightly. "Do you intend to dissect me like you do the fish?"

Koios stood with his hands behind his back and took a step forward.

"No. Again, let us observe the patterns and consider what they mean. You have a very similar form to myself and all other humans, yet your skin is much paler, your nails more claw-like, your teeth much sharper, and your ability to heal much faster. The differences are significant enough for me to know that you are unique, but not so dissimilar to make me think that you are a lesser creature. While animals may have similar reactions as humans to kindness and pain, you have also learned our language and are now exhibiting signs that your mind is capable of pondering what is both within and without, much like a human."

Wyrm paused. What the old man said made sense but still seemed strange. He turned, sat back down in a corner of his cage, and stared off into space. The old man returned to his table and his dissections.

"If you think I'm like you, then why do you keep me caged and chained?"

The old man didn't turn around. "That is another lesson: Make sure you learn from what you observe and do not make the same mistakes. The traders who sold you to me informed me of your violent outbursts, which is why they chained you as they did. I then observed how you were so enraged by Aurelia's cruelty that you were willing to damage yourself in order to hurt her, even to the point where it might have killed you. Such behaviors lead me to believe that you are prone to being controlled by your rage and bitterness, and that you do not value reason or peace. While I am delighted to learn more about you through conversation, it would be unwise of me to allow you too much freedom, lest your rage lead to my own death."

Wyrm wasn't sure if the old man was being condescending, but the dismissal of his righteous fury in regard to Aurelia's cruelty rekindled his rage. He stood quickly and stepped toward the bars. "Why shouldn't I be angry? Why shouldn't I kill those who torment me?!"

The old man sighed, placed his palms on the table, and leaned into them. "There are various philosophical and religious reasons that people do not hurt others, even those who hurt them. Some place a high value on human life, while others focus on seeing the world from the perspective of others. There is even a new religion spreading across the Empire that encourages its adherents to love their enemies. If nothing else, consider what is in your own best interest. Killing or permanently damaging yourself is not helpful for you in the long run. If you are patient and control yourself, you can avoid unnecessary harm to yourself, and you may be able to achieve something greater in the future. The more you achieve, the less past wrongs will bother you."

Wyrm glared at the old man. He still saw no reason to care for these humans, and especially no reason to love an enemy, but he could see the value in waiting if it got him what he wanted. Perhaps he should give more consideration to patience.

*   *   *

A few years went by, and Wyrm learned as much as he could from Koios and Aurelia. He even allowed them to cut him and time how long it took for his wounds to heal. The pain still angered him, but over time, he was able to better control it. The more well fed he was, the faster he healed. While learning more about his abilities was fascinating, he still did not trust them, especially Aurelia. Wyrm would wait for her to leave before engaging Koios in conversation. His newfound eagerness to learn encouraged him to speak to the old man, but his bitterness kept him silent before the girl. Oddly enough, it seemed like Koios respected this decision, as Aurelia never showed any signs that the old man had told her

55

about their conversations.

For a time, Aurelia's visits became much less frequent, but eventually she returned. One night, she arrived in the darkness with several armed guards. They used loops of rope on the ends of long poles to move Wyrm from his cage to another, smaller cage outside. He was forced into this new container, and a cover was placed over it. He didn't know where they went, but when the cover was removed, he found himself in an empty marble room.

The room was rectangular with a marble pedestal and bowl at one end, and several holes through which his chains fed were on the other. The guards left and Aurelia entered. She stood near the door in the center of one of the side walls.

"This will be your new home. You will notice that your chains can allow you to move freely, but they can also be pulled through those holes so that you are unable to move." She looked over her shoulder toward the open doorway, nodded, and Wyrm felt the chains and his body being pulled back toward the wall. She raised her hand and it stopped.

Aurelia gestured toward the marble bowl, and Wyrm noticed a pipe protruding from the wall above the bowl. "We will supply you with blood through there. As long as you cooperate, your chains will be loose, and you will be well fed."

Wyrm looked at her. She seemed slightly older now and more serious. In the cage in Koios's home, it was hard to measure the passage of time, and Wyrm began to wonder how many years had passed.

*   *   *

Aurelia entered the temple from a secret entrance behind the large statue of the temple's deity. It was a strange mix of human and animal, though it was predominantly snake and human. Her face was concealed behind a mask formed in the likeness of a human-snake hybrid with noticeably large fangs. Her robes were a deep dark red, reminiscent of dried blood. She looked past the base supporting the statue at the assembled worshipers.

The temple was a long rectangle, extending away from the idol with pillars spaced out along either side. The majority of the worshipers were arrayed between the two rows of pillars, in the open space, all face down before the deity's image. An altar had been placed in front of the idol, and both stood on a raised platform several steps higher than where the majority of the worshipers were positioned. On either side of the altar were hooded figures, all wearing red cloaks in contrast to the white cloaks of those below.

Aurelia made her way to her place between the idol and the altar, careful to avoid the steps that descended directly in front of the idol to the cult's second circle of chambers. On the other side of the altar, a young woman knelt on the steps of the dais, the newest candidate for the cult's inner circle.

"Welcome child. Are you prepared to step from the third circle into the second circle of devotion?" Aurelia asked, looking down at the woman's bowed head.

"Yes. Please accept these two prime slaves as sacrifice to show my devotion to our cause."

Two blindfolded slaves were then brought forth; one man and one woman. They were forced down onto their knees on either side of the altar.

"Our master requires our obedience and devotion in both life and death," Aurelia declared. She grabbed the man's hair, slit his throat, and shoved the bleeding gash toward the bowel-shaped depression in the center of the altar.

As the male slave ceased moving, Aurelia turned to the

woman and cut her blindfold.

"This man's death serves our master, as your life will now serve him."

The guards came and carried the woman down the set of steps in front of the idol leading into the inner chambers of the cult.

Aurelia stepped around the altar, placed her hand in the blood, then looked down at the supplicant.

"Look at me," she commanded.

The young woman looked up and immediately Aurelia's blood-covered hand gripped her throat, fingers curling in around the trachea and between the tendons, her sharpened fingernails making small cuts in the skin.

Aurelia glared into the woman's eyes, relishing slightly the fear she could see in them. "Let this blood and these marks forever remind you that your life is in my hands, and my hands serve the master."

"I am forever bound," replied the woman as she closed her eyes.

*   *   *

Wyrm instinctively knew what time it was and walked across the barren stone room to the pipe and the bowel below. After a few minutes, blood began to pour out. He eagerly lapped it from the bowel until the flow stopped.

It was human blood. He could tell by the rush of energy and strength he felt whenever he drank it. Aurelia had previously noticed the changes in his demeanor when he was fed human instead of animal blood. She later explained that the blood came from the sacrifices of the cult she ran. It was not lost on him that her ability to deduce this was due to his lack of self-control over his more subtle characteristics, and that her telling him was her way of demonstrating that he could not hide things from her. This had motivated him to work more to conceal his true feelings; yet, with the general boredom of sitting in a stone box with nothing to do, he would forget frequently.

The long expanses of time between feedings left Wyrm little else to do other than to alternate between mentally shutting down while staring off into space and contemplating the things he'd observed and learned when he lived in Koios's cage. As a result, he would reach valuable conclusions but would then lose the drive and motivation to make anything of them.

After some time, the chains bound to the spiked shackles around his neck, wrists, and ankles began to pull him, and he walked back to the far side of the room and sat down.

Aurelia entered a moment later followed by a guard and a rather frightened-looking slave girl.

"You may leave us," Aurelia commanded the guard, who bowed obediently, left, and closed the door behind him.

"You will be rewarded if you assist me with a series of experiments," she continued.

"What kind of experiments?" Wyrm asked cautiously, looking the visitor up and down. Her hair was dark, her body neither emaciated nor plump. He could see that her hands were only lightly calloused, and her eyes looked at things intently. Perhaps, he thought, she was a more educated slave and not one used for hard labor or previously owned by a harsh master.

"I would like to examine the full range of your abilities and characteristics. Some of these experiments may require the examination of your blood, and others will require you to utilize your abilities."

"Well, I don't appear to be going anywhere any time

soon, so I have plenty of time, but... I am curious as to how this would benefit me," Wyrm replied.

"The more one learns of one's own abilities, the more one can accomplish. Also, you will no longer need to feed on the stale remnants of our ceremonies. You will have fresh meals."

At this, the slave looked fearfully between Aurelia and him. He wondered what horrible thoughts were racing through her mind.

"That sounds reasonable. What is her name?"

"Let's call her, 'One.'" Aurelia turned and walked to the door. The guard opened it, and as Aurelia stepped through the doorway, she called back over her shoulder, "Your first experiment, is to drain her."

Wyrm felt the chains go slack as the door latched shut and the bar was placed across it. He stood and took a step toward the girl. She backed away from him, and he smiled.

This would be fun, he thought. It would give him something to do and something to ponder, especially since he wasn't fully sure of his own limits.

Wyrm dashed to the woman, gripped her shoulders, and sank his teeth into her throat. The blood poured out, and he gulped it down greedily. He was barely aware of her feeble attempts at breaking free of his grasp.

Eventually, the blood stopped, and Wyrm became aware of his surroundings again. The woman in his hands was dead. He let her body drop to the floor as he closed his eyes. The power coursing through him was something he had not experienced in many years. This much fresh human blood made him feel like he could take on the world, and nothing could stop him. He clenched his hand into a fist, one finger at a time, his mind caressing the chains behind him, wondering if he could break them.

Wyrm sighed. It would be best to wait. Even if he could break free, it would not do for Aurelia to find out before he was ready.

He looked down at the lifeless corpse. He knew what would happen but had never taken the time to closely observe it before.

Wyrm sat back down, leaning against the wall, his right arm resting on his raised right knee, and stared at the corpse expectantly.

Eventually the corpse twitched.

*   *   *

Aurelia made her way around the perimeter of the creature's newest chamber. Unlike the last one, this one had a series of smaller rooms evenly spaced along the length of the rectangle with the main entrance on one end and the retractable chains on the other. There were five cells on either side, each housing, or soon to house, a specimen for experimentation. Grooves ran along the floor from each cell and down toward a depression in the floor near the chains so that any excess blood would be available for the creature to feed on.

There were also five stone tables fitted with chains and spiked shackles arranged end to end down the center of the room. Grooves in them also led to the creature's feeding trough.

She looked through the bars at the newest test subject, recently branded '57.' The subject was significantly older than most of her test subjects. He was a blind beggar that no one would miss.

Aurelia made a gesture, and a guard opened the cell, pulled the man out, dragged him to a table, and chained him down. She nodded, and the guard left the room and closed the door.

"What is the experiment for today?" asked the creature from his seat on the floor at the far end of the room.

Aurelia brought forth a small vial of the creature's blood from a pouch on her belt and opened it. "We're going to test the extent of the restorative power of your blood on a living, non-transformed specimen."

She dispensed three drops of the red liquid into the eyes of the old blind man and watched. She had seen the blood heal lacerations on contact and expected something similar, but nothing happened.

"Perhaps his eyes do not heal, because his body is not trying to repair damage to them right now," offered the creature.

Aurelia paused and considered. This was a good suggestion, and the creature had steadily shown more aptitude and helpfulness in her experiments, but his ability to so clearly see what was going on from such a distance was somewhat worrisome. She was pleased that she had decided to always keep the creature in check and restrained when she was in the room with him.

With one swift movement, Aurelia drew a large needle from her belt and stabbed the old man's right eye. He screamed and fought against his chains. Aurelia grabbed his head, pried his eye open, dripped three more drops of blood into the damaged eye, and watched it heal. The man's thrashing stopped, and his newly restored eye turned toward her and glared.

"Excellent suggestion. Do you think there may be a way to restore his whole body without inflicting wounds on him?"

"Perhaps the restorative powers interact with the

subject's own blood when there is a wound or with the healing process itself. If the blood doesn't restore from being poured over the eye, perhaps it is because it is merely contacting the surface of things and not the interior. How best should we transfer the blood to the interior of the subject?"

Aurelia mused over this; "We could attempt to inject it into the bloodstream as a snake does its venom, or we could see what happens when ingested" She grabbed the old man's head, inserted a device to hold his mouth open, and poured the rest of the blood into his mouth.

She stepped back and watched. There was no immediate change, but even the creature had taken time to heal when she had first met him, so perhaps the same would hold true now.

It would be best to have a more precise way to measure and test the injection methods. Her one concern was that ingesting the blood, or even injecting too much, might cause a complete transformation. The goal was to take the creature's power without its weaknesses. She walked away and indicated at the door for the guard to enter and return the subject to his cell.

*   *   *

Wyrm sat and watched from his end of the room, staring at the five newest subjects all chained down to the stone tables in preparation for Aurelia's daily studies. He thought they were numbers 87 through 91. He had transformed all of them a few days ago, and they had been fed daily with human blood. Aurelia's newest set of tests were designed to look for weaknesses of the creatures, since she had already learned how to steal some of their strengths.

By this point, it had been several years since he'd last

63

spent time among people, but he was still fairly certain that Aurelia should have been showing more signs of aging by this point than she was. He knew she'd developed a glass vial with measured markings attached to a hollow metal spike so that she could inject measured amounts of his blood into her. This was most likely slowing her aging as well as enhancing her strength.

Wyrm had been rather surprised at her display of genuine elation the day she came in and explained how she had been angered by a guard and lifted him off the ground with one hand. He wasn't sure what other advantages the blood was giving her, but he secretly hoped it did not impart all of his growing abilities.

Having seen the blood's benefits, Aurelia was looking to make sure she didn't inherit any weaknesses.

His thoughts were interrupted by Aurelia storming into the room with an exceptionally irritated look on her normally stoic visage. He watched as she walked to the subject on the first table. She began lacerating the subject and pouring various substances into the wounds to observe how the flesh reacted. Her movements were unusually rushed and frustrated, lacking the meticulousness that they usually possessed.

"Has something gone wrong?" he asked.

"This is all that bastard's fault," she growled as she plunged the knife deep into the creature's chest.

"Your husband? Has he done something? Has he lost status? I thought you said he'd risen quite successfully through the ranks."

Aurelia turned and glared at him; "The bastard got me pregnant. I can't risk continuing to take the blood in case it causes a mutation in the child. I don't want one of these creatures growing inside me and clawing its way out. If I can't take the blood, that leaves me vulnerable to attack, or even to being replaced if the effects of the pregnancy deteriorate my appearance enough that he decides to move on to a younger, more politically beneficial bride."

Wyrm restrained a smile at Aurelia's frustration. It was an unusual sight for him.

"If I remember our previous conversations accurately, your husband has risen through the ranks by virtue of his own honor and benevolence, combined with your secret machinations. He is intelligent enough to be good at his occupation, but not so cunning as to contemplate the less honorable aspects of politics and rule. With that in mind, I find it unlikely that he would replace you."

He watched as the anger began to ease out of Aurelia's face while she stood over the test subject, staring blankly at it.

"Besides, should the pregnancy damage you, you could always cut the child out of you and pour the blood in the wound as a quick fix."

This seemed to alleviate her final wisps of anger. Wyrm smiled inwardly. He could see both the external signs of her acceptance of the situation as well as images of the contingency plans forming in her mind.

*   *   *

Aurelia held her child for the first time and felt as if she had never even been capable of thinking about this beautiful creature as anything other than the most important thing in her life. Several weeks passed where she spent all her time with her new daughter, ignoring all other duties and goals.

Despite her newfound devotion, Aurelia eventually returned to her role as dutiful wife and covert high priestess. Years passed and her followers grew in number, rank, and utility.

"My Lady," a red-cloaked devotee said as he knelt before Aurelia in one of the inner chambers of the cult.

She looked out through the eyes of her mask, down at the young soldier whose true loyalties were contained within the walls of the room in which they stood.

"Tell me, has your general made his decision on whether or not he intends to march his forces to the capital?"

"He has. We march in two days."

"Such blatant arrogance is an affront to the wishes of our master," Aurelia replied, reaching into her robes and producing a small vial. "Pour this into his wine tonight, so he may taste our master's displeasure."

"As the master wishes, and as you so command." The guard accepted the vial and, with head bowed, left.

Aurelia made her way back through the secret tunnels to her chambers in her husband's estate, leaving her ceremonial robes and mask behind. It was time for her to check with her daughter Julia's tutors.

None of the tutors she could find lived up to Koios's legacy, so she had hired three of them to try making up the difference. She strode purposefully into the chamber where the tutors were waiting.

"Give me your reports," she said as she took her seat and the three tutors knelt before her.

"Your daughter has surpassed my expectations in mathematics and natural philosophy for one as young as her," replied the first tutor, an older, slender man with graying hair.

"Excellent." She turned to the second.

"Her grasp of history and geography is progressing quite nicely. Her questions are probing and insightful," reported the second tutor, a middle-aged man with a slight limp from an imperfectly healed battle wound.

"Good."

"Her reading and reasoning skills are quite developed for a 10-year-old child," remarked the third tutor, a middle-aged woman with the faintest hints of gray showing in her hair.

"I am pleased with your reports," Aurelia stated. "Is she still holding on to this imaginary friend of hers?"

"The 'man with the funny smile' has not been mentioned for quite some time," replied the third tutor. "We had many debates about the frivolity of imaginary friends. Eventually, she stopped talking about him, and, when asked, she says she no longer dreams of him."

"Thank you all for your service. Continue to excel in training my daughter, and your lives here will be quite pleasant."

The three tutors left.

*　　*　　*

The years passed and Aurelia watched her daughter grow into a beautiful and intelligent young woman.

"Mother, I have noticed that you have not aged as the mothers of my friends have," Julia commented while they sat together reading one day.

Aurelia set down her scroll and looked at her daughter. For a brief moment, she debated telling her daughter of her secrets.

"I have been gifted with slower aging, but I can feel age beginning to creep in these last few years." She wasn't fond of deceiving her daughter, but secrets only survived when they went unshared.

"How fortunate," Julia responded and continued reading.

67

Aurelia gently stroked the vial of Wyrm's blood that she wore around her neck and went back to her reading.

*   *   *

Aurelia watched her daughter converse with her friends in the courtyard. They were all smiles and laughter. She could see a lot of herself in Julia. Even now, she noticed that her daughter portrayed more playfulness among others than she did when they were alone.

"Mother, come show my friends some archery," she said, running up beside her.

"I'm not sure that is the sort of thing they would be interested in," Aurelia replied.

"Oh yes, please teach us."

"My father won't let me practice."

"OK," sighed Aurelia.

She made her way to the side of the courtyard and retrieved a bow and a few arrows. She demonstrated how to nock the arrow and took aim at a fruit on a tree several yards away. The arrow pierced the fruit and it fell.

"Oh, let me try."

"Be careful, this isn't a toy," warned Aurelia.

The first girl took aim and missed the tree entirely.

The second hit the tree.

Aurelia walked over to the tree to retrieve the arrows. She placed one hand on the trunk, well away from the arrow, and wrapped the fingers of her other hand around the shaft. As she began to pull, a slight sound caught her attention.

Without thought, Aurelia spun, her right hand releasing the trapped arrow and sweeping across the space in front of her head. She felt the edge of her hand contact something smooth and thin, beginning to push it aside. Her fingers wrapped around the object and she looked straight ahead.

Julia dropped the bow, a look of panic washing over her face. Her two friends were not paying attention. Aurelia looked down at her right hand and saw an arrow clutched there.

"I'm so sorry mother. It was an accident," pleaded Julia as she rushed to meet her.

Aurelia comforted her daughter and departed as soon as seemed appropriate.

When she returned to her chambers, she clenched her fist and snapped the arrow. How could she be so stupid. Eventually her daughter would figure out that she wasn't just gifted or lucky. Her mind and heart were torn between her desires to protect her daughter and to protect herself.

Giving up her power was unacceptable, but she could never manage a confrontation with her daughter. Her only option was to disappear from her daughter's life and live only in the shadows of the cult. That would allow her to retain and gain control in the Empire while protecting her daughter.

Having made up her mind, Aurelia set about preparations for a trip along the coast. Carriages fell off cliffs all the time.

*   *   *

The carriage raced along the road as the sun set. Aurelia opened a small box and extracted a glass vial of Wyrm's blood and a syringe of her own design. She drew out the blood and injected it into her veins.

The power surged through her. This was more than she usually used, but her tasks ahead would require the extra strength, and she didn't want to risk the effects wearing off too soon.

69

Faster than a human eye could follow, she opened the carriage door and climbed onto the roof. The sound caused the guard seated next to the driver to look back. She reached forward, grabbed him by the head, and threw him over the cliff.

The guard's screams caught the driver's attention. Before he could turn too far, Aurelia struck him across the back of the head in the direction away from the cliff and toward the road. He fell in a heap on the ground unconscious.

She climbed down and rushed along the backs of the horses to jump in front of them. As soon as she landed, she spun around and drew her dagger. The force of her fist, the slash of the blade, and her sudden appearance scared the horses, and they lurched toward her left and the cliff's edge. As they attempted to pass her, she gave a quick shove, and they tumbled over the edge.

*   *   *

The journey back had gone fairly quickly as Aurelia found herself able to move faster than the horses. She'd never fully tested the speed that Wyrm's blood bestowed over such long distances. It was exhilarating.

Once inside the cult's underground labyrinth, she began to relax. Living the rest of her life in such obscurity would be worth it once her reach extended to the capital. She didn't need to be in the spotlight, just to have control.

She made her way through the twisting passages until she reached the chambers of the high priestess of the cult. She unlocked the door and entered.

The opposite wall was lined with shelves containing hundreds of scrolls. Some were reports from her spies, others were recently written works by the philosophers, and others were her own records. To her left was a long table at which she would perform experiments, study the scrolls, or create her own. On the right was a small bed. Her red robes of office hung in the center of the shelves.

She reached to her right and felt only stone. Her robes weren't supposed to be by the shelves. She always hung them on the wrack to her right, but it was empty.

Instinctively, Aurelia clutched the handle of her dagger and stood with one foot forward, ready to pounce on her intruder.

"Who are you?"

The robes slowly turned around.

"Mother! I'm so glad you're alive," exclaimed Julia, a smile spreading across her face. "We were worried that something unfortunate might have happened on your journey."

Aurelia took a step back in surprise. How had Julia even found this place?

Her daughter walked forward to embrace her. Confusion froze Aurelia momentarily, and she allowed the embrace.

Julia looked at her and reached out to gently stroke Aurelia's face.

"Don't worry mother. I wanted to make sure I saw you at the height of your strength and beauty one last time."

Aurelia blinked as her daughter's words began to process. What did she mean by "we"? Something wasn't right. She quickly moved away from her daughter and looked around.

"What did you mean by 'we'?"

With a speed far greater than her human daughter should have been capable of, Julia closed the distance between them.

"How did you..." she began angrily when she felt the

cold slice across her throat.

Blood gurgled in her throat as Aurelia dropped to her knees.

"It's OK, mother. Soon you shall be at peace."

Wyrm walked out from the shadows and stood behind her daughter. Julia turned and greeted him with a hug.

"You have done well, my beautiful child," he said as he stroked her hair. "Now go prepare to meet your new congregation."

Julia kissed his cheek and left the room without looking back.

Wyrm crouched down next to Aurelia as she tried in vain to hold in the blood pouring from her neck. The wound was healing faster than normal, but not fast enough. Too much time had passed since the injection.

"I should thank you. You have taught me more than I ever could have imagined: academics, cunning, manipulation, ambition... and patience," he finished with an icy tone.

He reached out, dipped his finger in her blood, and brought it up to his face to examine. With one long lick his tongue wiped the blood clean from his finger.

"Your daughter is amazing, already so much more than you. Together, no empire can stand against us. You have been my captor and tormentor for years, but you have also been my teacher. For that, I offer you this one reprieve: peace."

With that, Wyrm reached out and snapped her neck. For one fleeting moment, she realized she could not feel her body any longer. The moment ended as the cracking sounds in her skull reached their climax.

IV

Eleanor
Dynoltir, +2003 TR

Donna awoke to the impact of a small yet sizable weight slamming into her and her husband.

"It's morning now! Daddy said we could go hiking in the morning!"

Donna reluctantly opened her eyes to see her daughter laying across her and trying to shake her husband awake. They were on a weekend camping trip, and Donna was beginning to second-guess her decision to not let Lucy have her own tent.

"Don't jump on your mother. Come on. Let's go hiking," Peter said groggily as he sat up.

Lucy reached for the zipper to the tent and screamed.

Donna sat bolt upright, fully awake in that instant. "What is it?!"

"There's a spider on the tent," Lucy said as she scurried back toward her parents.

Donna gave Peter a look and turned toward Lucy. "It's OK, the spider's more afraid of you than you are of it."

"Then it must be terrified and want me dead," retorted Lucy.

Peter laughed, crawled toward the tent, caught the spider, unzipped the flap, and threw it outside. "There, it's nowhere near us now."

"Thank you," Lucy said, giving her father a hug.

Donna watched them put on their shoes and light jackets.

"Have fun and be safe," she said as she watched them leave the tent.

"OK, Mommy, I love you. Bye, bye!" Lucy dashed off

out of sight, followed by her father.

Donna smiled and collapsed back into her sleeping bag. Time to get more sleep.

*   *   *

Donna finished getting dressed and exited the tent. The remnants of the previous night's campfire were about ten feet in front of her. The car was parked off to her right at the base of the dirt road that led out of this clearing in the national park. She closed her eyes, breathed in the scents of the forest, and listened for the sounds of distant birds. To her surprise, the forest was quiet. She'd been camping in this area before, and birds usually called out in the morning. She had looked forward to their songs on these trips.

Shrugging it off, Donna went about preparing breakfast. She knew that Lucy would be hungry when she got back from her hike, so she set about preparing some oatmeal.

She stood up from the camping stove to go get something from the car, turned, and saw Lucy standing on the edge of the clearing, covered in blood.

Donna's eyes went wide; "Lucy!" she shouted as she ran to her daughter, knelt down, and embraced her.

"Lucy? Are you OK? Are you hurt?"

Lucy just stared at her silently.

Donna's heart pounded in her chest as she examined Lucy for injuries but found none. She looked at Lucy's face to find only her blank stare.

Her mind raced to find some possible explanation for why her daughter would be uninjured yet covered in blood. A sharp stab of irritation passed at the notion that Peter should have taken better care of her. Guilt and worry flooded in next as she realized that Peter was nowhere to be seen.

74

"Where's Daddy?" she asked Lucy.

Lucy silently turned and pointed back up the trail into the forest.

Donna stood and hesitated. She was now desperately worried about her husband, but she didn't want to take her daughter closer to possible danger or leave her unprotected at the camp.

She scooped up Lucy and rushed back to the car. Once they were locked inside, Donna called the police and waited.

Tears burned her eyes as she fought not to cry in front of her daughter while myriad horrors of what probably happened rushed through her mind. She held her daughter as an eternity passed before the police arrived with an ambulance.

The paramedics checked out her and her daughter while the police searched the trails. Eventually they returned with news, coalescing her fears into one horrible reality. Her husband was dead, torn to pieces by some kind of wild animal.

Donna hugged her daughter close as the tears poured silently down her face.

*   *   *

Fred's mind lurched into consciousness as his body sat bolt upright. He shuddered as a sense of horror and disgust slowly faded from his mind. Looking around past the edge of his makeshift camp, he quickly dismissed the sensation as the lingering effects of a dream. He scratched his head and felt the fine grit of dirt from sleeping on the ground every night without being able to shower regularly. Sometimes he would use the restroom sinks in the park to clean himself up, but it had been several days since he last had the chance.

There was no one there, just the trees of the national

park. Usually a park ranger or police officer would wake him up, telling him he couldn't sleep here or trying to take him to the local homeless shelter.

His stomach growled, reminding him that he hadn't eaten for a long time. Fred rummaged around in his backpack only to find empty containers that he tossed casually to the ground. He needed to find food.

Fred stood, planning to make his way down to the restaurants and hotels outside the park. The nicer restaurants always threw out the best food.

But first, he needed to find something.

He wasn't sure what it was or why it was more important than food, but he did know that he needed to find it.

Fred stumbled to his feet. He needed to find it, so he began walking.

*   *   *

Donna looked to make sure Lucy was with her parents, then she excused herself from the group of people surrounding her husband's casket at the viewing. She made her way through the funeral home to an empty room, closed the door, and collapsed on the floor, letting out the sobs she had been struggling to hold in for the last couple hours.

After a few minutes, she silently berated herself for breaking down when Lucy had remained so calm.

A moment later, the door opened and Lucy walked into the room. Donna quickly wiped away her tears and turned toward her daughter.

Lucy walked over and hugged her, "it's OK, Mommy. We're safe now."

"Thank you," she said, hugging her back. "I miss Daddy a lot, and it makes me very sad. You know, if you need

76

to cry, you can. It's OK to cry sometimes."

Lucy looked at her, "I know, but I'm OK. I know we're safe now."

Donna hugged her daughter again. She got up, took Lucy by the hand, and returned to the viewing.

The days turned to weeks, and Donna found herself crying a little less each day. It helped that Lucy was so strong and comforting for her, but she was worried that Lucy never seemed to cry.

Donna was carrying laundry down the hall and could hear Lucy talking to someone in her room. She set down the basket quietly and approached the door but did not enter or show herself in the doorway.

"It's OK if Mommy is listening to us. I think she would like you if she just got to know you."

Donna's eyes went wide and she quickly spun into the doorway. Lucy was staring up at the corner of the ceiling and turned to her as she entered.

"Hi, Mommy."

"Who were you talking to?" she asked.

"I was talking to Eleanor. She's my best friend."

"Can I meet her?"

Lucy looked over her shoulder, up at the corner of the ceiling again, and her shoulders slumped slightly. "She's already left. I don't know why, but she's really shy around you. She doesn't think you will like her."

"Well, maybe sometime we can meet each other." Donna looked around the room, turned, and left.

She went back to putting away the laundry, pondering how concerned she should be about her daughter's imaginary friend.

Many children have imaginary friends at some point. It's perfectly normal and something that they eventually grow out of, right?

But how did she know that Donna was listening? Perhaps Lucy heard a board creak and was just playing around. She shrugged. It was probably nothing to worry about.

Donna walked back to Lucy's room to get her for supper. Lucy was sitting in the middle of the floor, playing with her toys. She smiled and watched her daughter for a few moments before movement caught her eye.

A large spider was scurrying across the floor toward Lucy's toys. Donna stopped leaning against the doorway and stood up, expecting the inevitable scream.

Lucy jerked slightly when she caught sight of the spider out of the corner of her eye but didn't scream. It was more like it had just startled her. Donna watched in amazement as Lucy calmly reached out her hand and let the spider climb onto it. As the spider moved from one side of her hand to the other, Lucy turned her hand and even brought up her other hand so that the spider would crawl from hand to hand.

The spider stopped on her palm and turned to face Lucy.

Lucy's head tilted to one side and she whispered, "Yes, you're right," before laying her hand on the floor and allowing the spider to scurry away to the other side of the room.

Donna walked into the room.

"You are a brave little girl. I thought you hated spiders."

"Eleanor says it's silly for me to be afraid of spiders."

"Is Eleanor here now?"

"No, not right now, but I can still hear her."

Donna looked around nervously.

"Come, it's time for supper," she said, guiding Lucy out of the room and giving it one last suspicious look before she left.

*   *   *

Donna sat outside on the patio watching Lucy play in the backyard. The yard was surrounded by a low brick wall that was about as tall as Lucy. There was a line of bushes along the back edge that separated in the center to allow for the back gate. A tree stood in each corner, and a couple more lined each side along the wall as it led back to the house. She no longer allowed her daughter to play outside alone or be anywhere unattended, and the surrounding foliage made her feel protected yet vulnerable at the same time.

Lucy was chatting away pleasantly to her invisible friend while staring at the bushes in the corner of the yard. Donna smiled to herself and looked down at her book.

A few minutes went by and she looked up again, but Lucy was gone.

Donna shot out of her chair, throwing the book aside as she rushed toward the corner of the yard.

"Lucy!"

She reached the bushes and started frantically pulling back the branches.

A stick broke behind her, "what's wrong? Why are you shouting?"

Donna spun around to find Lucy stepping out from the other end of the bushes dressed in a fine silk dress with a silk ribbon around her neck. Donna's eyes widened, "Where did you get that dress?"

"Eleanor made it for me. Isn't it pretty?" Lucy said as she spun around.

"Yes..."

Donna stood up straighter and began looking around.

79

She went to the bushes that Lucy had just exited but saw no signs of anyone on the other side.

"You know what, sweety, I think we should go visit your grandma."

"OK."

Donna picked up Lucy, walked through the house, grabbed her purse and keys, and went straight to the car. She buckled Lucy in the passenger seat and went around to the driver's side. Her hands shook as she pulled out her keys and started the car. She reversed into the street, changed gears, and took off.

Fear and worry swirled through Donna's head as she drove to her parents' house. Where had that dress come from? Was Eleanor real, were they being stalked? What had it done to her husband and to her daughter?

Questions filled her head as they drove on. Her parents lived a couple hours away, so hopefully she'd have a safe distance between her daughter and whatever this Eleanor really was.

"If we go to Grandma's, will Eleanor still be able to find me?"

"No."

"Then I don't know that I want to go to Grandma's. Eleanor's my friend, and I will miss her."

"Eleanor is not your friend, and I don't want you to speak of her again."

"Eleanor is too my friend!"

"Shut up about Eleanor and stop lying to me," she yelled.

Donna glanced over to see Lucy glaring at her with folded arms and the faintest hints of moisture in her eyes. She turned back to the road and kept driving.

*   *   *

Fred's eyes blinked open, and the branches of a bush slowly gained focus near his head. He was lying on his left side, his back next to something cold and hard. He looked around, confused as to why he was sleeping under a bush next to a low brick wall that appeared to surround someone's backyard. His mind raced through his memories, searching for some clue as to how he got there, but found nothing.

A strange, wet, sticky feeling greeted his hands as he pushed himself up into a sitting position. Looking down, his eyes went wide with horror as he realized that the ground and much of his clothing was covered in blood. Fear and panic swept across him and he groped his body, searching for wounds, but found none.

Fred heaved a sigh of relief and looked to his right. The mangled remains of a corpse drained all relief from him. He scrambled to back away from it. His pulse quickened as his adrenaline surged. If he was found now, he would be doomed. He had no idea how this person was killed or why their blood was all over him, but people tended to not trust homeless people, even when they weren't covered in blood.

A shiver ran up his spine and he felt the fear fade. There was something that he needed to find; something close by. He could sense that it had been here only recently. The idea of having just missed his target was both frustrating and exhilarating. He would have it soon.

Fred stood up, oblivious to the branches scraping across his skin, and stumbled through them into the yard. He made his way up the steps of the patio, barely noticing the carelessly discarded book as his foot collided with it. He entered the house.

81

*   *   *

"I don't know what to do, Mom," Donna said as she sat across the kitchen table from her mother. She and Lucy had been living with them for about a week, but things kept getting worse.

"Lucy won't stop talking about this 'Eleanor' person. I'm worried that something bad might happen."

"Lots of children have imaginary friends. There's no harm in that," replied her mother.

"But I don't think she's imaginary," whispered Donna. "The dress was real. Something horrible happened in that forest, and I think someone is stalking my daughter."

Donna's mother reached out a hand to her but stopped at a sound from the doorway.

"I need to go back. Eleanor needs to find me," said Lucy standing in the doorway.

Donna turned toward her daughter, the mental exhaustion of everything tempting her to respond harsher than she knew she should.

"No, she doesn't," she said through gritted teeth.

"Something bad is coming, and Eleanor is worried that she won't be able to get to me in time if she doesn't know where I am," pleaded Lucy.

Donna turned her whole body to face her daughter. "I don't want you talking to or about Eleanor anymore."

Lucy glared back at her and replied in an icy voice, "Dad died in front of me, and you want to take away my only friend. I hate you and hope you die too." Lucy stormed off down the hallway.

Donna was speechless. Memories of Peter flooded her mind and constricted her throat while Lucy's words tore a jagged gash across her heart. She collapsed into sobs, barely aware of her mother rushing around the table and putting her arm around her as the pain overwhelmed her.

*   *   *

Donna loaded the groceries into the back of the car as Lucy watched her silently. Her daughter's quietness was somewhat disturbing, but at least she wasn't talking about Eleanor.

She returned the cart to the corral and turned to see Lucy waiting patiently in the passenger seat.

On the ride home, she decided to try talking to her daughter.

"Are you enjoying spending time with Grandpa and Grandma?" she asked.

After several moments of silence, she took a quick glance to see her daughter just staring straight ahead.

"What do you want for dinner?"

Again, silence.

They continued this way until they arrived at her parents' house.

"Come help with the groceries," Donna said.

Lucy obediently took the two lighter bags that Donna handed her, and they made their way inside.

Donna made her way up the front porch steps, shifting the bags to one hand and readying her house key. As she looked up to put it in the lock, she noticed the door was ajar.

Quietly setting the bags down, Donna guided Lucy to one side of the doorway, holding her finger over her mouth as a sign of silence.

She crept into the house as stealthily as possible.

The first two rooms were empty with no signs of trouble. When she reached the kitchen, she saw it.

83

There was blood everywhere. On the floor were the mangled bodies of her parents. Donna clapped her hands over her mouth to stifle her scream as her throat tightened and tears stung her eyes.

A small hand touched her back and she jumped, turning to see Lucy standing there looking up at her.

"I told you something bad was coming. I'm sorry you had to see this." Lucy's tone was eerily calm and sounded as if she was trying to be comforting, but the words and the situation made it much less so.

Donna scooped up her daughter and hurried out of the house. "I'm sorry you had to see that," she managed to choke out through her tears.

"It's OK. I've seen worse: when Daddy died," Lucy said calmly.

Donna's knees buckled and she barely managed to keep moving toward the car, as the tears blinded her and her throat tightened more than she could bear.

*   *   *

Donna returned home from work and walked up the steps toward the front porch. Several years had passed since the death of her parents, yet she had only recently realized that somewhere in that expanse of time she'd finally stopped looking over her shoulder and catching her breathe every time she unlocked the front door.

She walked inside and reflexively locked the door behind her. Her home was nothing special, neither exceptionally old nor brand new, but it had served as a fine place to raise her daughter on the far side of the country from where everything had fallen apart.

Finding a job had been hard at first, but eventually

84

everything fell into place. Lucy went to counseling and was put on medication until she stopped raving about Eleanor. After a few years of more normalized behavior, Lucy was weaned off the meds. So much time had gone by since then that Donna sometimes forgot her daughter ever even had an imaginary friend.

Once she grew accustomed to their new home, Lucy slowly began to excel in school. It was now her senior year, and she'd spent half of it openly debating with herself as to what her major should be. Donna shook her head as she remembered the excited conversations earlier that year.

"OK, Mom, which sounds more interesting: liquids that become solids under tension and are stronger than steel... or the physics of how gravity works so that we can use it to warp space-time to create wormholes?"

"Whichever one makes you happiest," Donna replied.

Lucy rolled her eyes, "Ugh, that's not helpful," and wandered back to her room.

Donna smiled at the memory and sighed. That excitement seemed gone as of late. She didn't know what was going on, but Lucy seemed quieter and somewhat sad. It hurt when Lucy just shrugged it off each time she asked what was wrong.

Some habits die hard, and she found herself standing in the hallway, watching her daughter for several moments before speaking.

"Good afternoon, honey. How was your day?"

Lucy turned around, and Donna noticed the same slumped shoulders and fake smile as Lucy replied, "It was OK"

"I was just about to make supper. What would you like?"

Lucy shrugged, "I don't care. I need to go finish some

homework and take a shower. Sorry."

Donna watched her daughter walk quietly up the stairs to her bedroom.

*   *   *

Lucy dropped her backpack next to her desk and closed her bedroom door. She slumped onto her bed and stared off into space.

The walls and bookshelves ceased to register in her consciousness as it shifted its focus to the empty sadness she felt inside. She thought through her life; her grades were good, she had fun with her friends, her mom didn't hassle her about things, and she'd gotten accepted to the college of her dreams...

But something was missing. She tilted her head slightly. There was this vague sense that she'd lost someone, like a close friend, but when she thought back on her memories, there was nothing. No memories of a friend she once had, nothing but a hollow void.

Lucy blinked and came back to the present. She looked around her room and realized she'd been sitting there for the better part of an hour. Her mind now rooted in the moment, she went about her normal activities.

Sometimes she'd come home and just sit, stare into space, and feel the empty sadness. Sometimes she'd cry and sometimes just stare. These times helped her hide her sadness when she was with her mother, at school, and with her friends. No one knew, but no one needed to know.

Lucy blinked and came back to reality, realizing she'd started staring off into space at her desk. She looked around her room. It was much darker now than when she'd gotten home. Her homework was finished, so she got ready for bed.

86

Lucy was eager for the oblivion of sleep, as it was better than being awake.

Sometimes, in her dreams, she was happy.

*   *   *

Weeks passed and graduation grew steadily nearer for Lucy. She stared at the food on her tray as she sat in the cafeteria with her friends at school.

"I'm so excited for graduation."

"I can't wait to meet my roommate. Meeting new people is one of the best things about going to college."

"I know. It really opens your eyes to new ideas and experiences."

Lucy barely heard all the excited chatter. More recently, she sometimes had brief lapses in her sorrow. It was as if she was happy that she'd found something long lost, but she felt confused by the notion.

"I'm looking forward to the job I'll get after I get my degree. Computer science is fascinating, pays well, and I might even be able to retire early."

"I know teaching won't pay well, but I still want to go into it. Helping future generations learn and grow is important so they can do great things."

Lucy closed her eyes and relaxed her mind, waiting for the answer to leap out of her subconscious as things sometimes did during tests or when waiting for inspiration. She sighed and poked at her food as the dark corners of her mind failed to offer any answers to her silent queries.

"What about you, Lucy? Did you decide what you're going to major in?"

Lucy's head snapped up and she flashed what was hopefully a disarming smile. "I think I'll wait till after the first semester to decide. I'm going to take a class or two of a few options and see which one I like best after that."

"That makes sense."

"Hey Lucy, the rest of us were going to hang out after school today. Do you want to join us?"

"No thanks, I have a lot of end of the year projects to finish. Thanks for asking though."

One by one, her friends got up and left. When they were gone, she let go of her smile and returned to her thoughts.

Lucy absentmindedly made her way to the gym for her next class when she walked into police tape. She looked up to see several police cars and an ambulance surrounding the maintenance shed next to the gym.

"What's going on?" she asked a nearby student.

"A teacher found the janitor dead in the maintenance shack."

Lucy looked around and saw one of her teachers sitting in the back of an ambulance. A police officer approached her and began asking questions. The teacher's body language became excited as she spoke to the officer before she suddenly turned away and lurched, vomiting all over the ground.

*   *   *

The superintendent decided to close the school for the day and send the students home. Lucy called her mom to let her know what happened and that she was safe.

"Go right home and lock the doors. I'm going to leave work early to come and stay with you," her mother said, panic in her voice.

"Mom, I'm OK. No one even tried to hurt any of the students today. There's no need to worry. I'll be fine. I'll call

88

you when I get home."

Her mother sighed; "Maybe you're right... but I still want you to call as soon as you get home, so I know you're safe. If there's a murderer out there, I don't want to take any chances."

"I will. I love you, goodbye," Lucy finished as she hung up the phone.

Her trip home was uneventful, as was the checking of every door and window when she called her mom. It wasn't until she'd reassured her mother for the umpteenth time that she finally relented and hung up.

The rest of the day was just as boring: homework, dinner, TV, and then a shower.

Lucy stepped out of the shower with a towel wrapped around her and walked into her room. A slight sound caught her attention, and she turned to look at the open window on the far side of the room.

Two long, segmented objects reached in through the window on either side and began probing the air. They curled into her room, and more segmented limbs began to poke through the window. The segmented limbs raised into view the head of a creature with large fangs that pointed down and toward each other while attached to a head with eight eyes.

Lucy stared in at the giant spider as it pulled itself through the window and into her room. Her mind raced back to her childhood. Images of spiders and the sounds of her own terrified screams flashed across her mind. The memories grew heavy and dark as she remembered the mangled body of her father lying on the ground in a pool of blood and torn flesh at her feet. Her young eyes lifted from the sight of her father's corpse to look straight into the eyes of a large spider just a few feet away on the other side.

Lucy's mind slammed back into the present as she

stared once more into that giant spider's lidless eyes.

Her mouth dropped open, and she screamed.

"Eleanor!"

Lucy rushed toward the giant spider and hugged it. All of her childhood memories came rushing back to her, and she knew what she'd missed and what she'd recently rediscovered. The realization washed over Lucy's mind that she had been recently sensing Eleanor's excitement as the spider had gotten closer to her.

*   *   *

Donna leaned on the kitchen counter drinking her morning coffee. She enjoyed the peaceful quiet of these morning moments before Lucy got up for school.

The sounds of hurried feet heralded the coming of her daughter. Much to her surprise, Donna looked up to see a smiling, energetic version of her daughter enter the kitchen and grab cereal for breakfast.

Smiling in relief and joy at her daughter's improved mood, Donna commented, "You're in a good mood this morning."

Lucy turned and smiled at her mother as she grabbed milk from the refrigerator and turned toward the kitchen table.

"Did you hear back from another college? I thought you were already accepted by the ones you wanted."

Lucy shook her head side to side and returned the milk to the fridge.

Narrowing her eyes, Donna asked, "Is it a boy?"

"Ha!" Lucy rolled her eyes and ate her breakfast.

Donna watched as Lucy ate her breakfast in record time. "Come on, tell me, what is it?"

"Oh, it's nothing," Lucy replied, tossing her bowl in

the sink before she dashed out of the house to school.

*   *   *

A couple days passed and Donna was feeling optimistic about the future. Lucy had been in the best mood she'd seen from her in years. She didn't know what had caused it, but at this point, she didn't care.

Graduation was only a couple weeks away, and Lucy's happy energy had infected Donna, prompting her to begin preparations for the open house they'd have after the graduation ceremony.

Donna's musings distracted her from her usual caution, and she opened the front door as soon as she heard the knock.

She stepped back in shock at the sight of a filthy, disheveled man in tattered clothes standing on her front porch. He was unshaven, uncombed, and looked and smelled like he hadn't showered in years. His eyes were blood shot, the lids half closed, with dark circles underneath.

The man stumbled forward as if compelled beyond unimaginable fatigue to keep moving.

Her eyes drifted to the dark stains on his chin that ran down the front of his shirt and jacket. They almost looked like dried blood.

Rancid breath poured over her face as he lurched closer; "I'm so tired. Please, tell me you have it, tell me you know what it is... I... I can't keep doing this."

*   *   *

"Lucy!" her teacher shouted as she slammed a book on her desk.

Lucy's head spun away from the window and she

91

stared at the teacher with what she knew was a dumb expression. "What?"

"I know you're close to graduation, but you still need to pay attention." The teacher glared at Lucy as she walked back toward the front of the room.

I'm sorry I caused you trouble, came Eleanor's thoughts.

It's not your fault, Lucy's mind responded. *I should have been paying more attention. It's just so good to finally see and talk to you again; I got carried away.*

The same is true for me. I should have known better. I will wait until after your classes have ended for the day.

You don't have to... I can split my attention.

Lucy sighed, as silence greeted her mind.

The rest of the day dragged on for an eternity. When the final bell rang, she ran out of school as fast as she could, mentally calling to Eleanor. They continued their excited conversation as she made her way home.

As Lucy approached her home, Eleanor sent her a warning.

Stop! Something's wrong. I sense something familiar, but different.

Images of something horrible happening to her mother flashed across her imagination, and Lucy ran the rest of the way home. She shot up the front porch steps and burst through the open door.

Lucy skidded to a halt when she faced a homeless man menacing her mother with a knife.

"Tell me where it is!" he pleaded and threatened.

"Get away from my mother!" Lucy shouted.

The homeless man turned and looked at Lucy.

"Finally!" he said with a sigh of relief.

"Run!" shouted Lucy's mother.

The man's body slumped and his eyes closed as if he was finally able to rest for the first time in years.

A giant, six-foot long centipede seemed to fade into existence as it crawled out of the homeless man and began to scurry across the floor toward Lucy. She held her ground, gripping the straps of her backpack as a weapon.

"Eleanor!"

A shimmering circular outline appeared in the air, and reality opened up like a trapdoor. Eleanor leaped out of the shimmering tunnel and attacked the giant centipede.

Lucy's mother ran past the fighting creatures and grabbed her, trying to pull her to the door. "We have to leave."

Lucy pulled away. "No, I have to help her."

She ran across the room and picked up the knife that the man had dropped. She turned and stabbed the centipede. It flailed in pain, ripping the knife from her grasp, and threw Eleanor across the room.

The centipede turned its attention to Lucy. She took a step back, but it was too late. The centipede spiraled around her body and reared its head over her. Its jaws opened as it prepared to bite her head off.

Eleanor sprang across the room, wrapped her legs around both of them, and sunk her fangs into the back of the centipede's head. The centipede twitched and writhed, unable to free itself. Eleanor's venom paralyzed the centipede and she crushed its head. The pair fell backward to the floor as strength drained from the centipede's body.

Lucy disentangled herself and turned to begin examining Eleanor to make sure she wasn't hurt.

"Lucy, get away from that thing," her mother said, grabbing her shoulder.

Lucy turned with a reassuring smile, "It's OK, Mom. This is Eleanor. She is my dearest friend. And she will always protect me."

*   *   *

Several years ago...

She sat and waited. She knew her prey would pass by soon. The wall in front of her shimmered slightly, but she could still sense what was on the other side. The shimmering silk was woven into a fine mesh all around her, creating a little pocket in space where she could hide.

Sounds caught her attention. Two humans were approaching. One of them was an adult male. The other was a small female child. The child seemed happy. She was talking excitedly to the adult male as they made their way along a path. She could sense the adult's tired yet happy responses to the child's exuberance.

Skimming through the minds of the humans distracted her momentarily. Too late, she sensed her prey at the same time that she sensed the pain in the adult male.

She shot through the trap door in space and landed on the first of the two large centipedes, sinking her fangs into its head and crushing it. The second centipede quickly attacked her. They fought viciously, but eventually she was able to kill it too.

She looked around. The adult human was dead, torn to pieces. His blood was everywhere. The human child was covered in blood as well. The child was in shock, staring at the corpse of the adult male.

She turned her attention to the child. The child's obvious emotional distress cut into her heart, drawing her full attention, so she did not see a much smaller centipede, about a foot long, scurry away under a rock.

She reached out with her mind to the child. She chose

a name from the child's memories.

My name is Eleanor. I mean you no harm.

Eleanor walked over and reached out an arm to stroke the child's hair in an attempt to comfort her. The child looked up from the bloody corpse of her father and stared into Eleanor's large round eyes.

I'm sorry about what happened to your father. If you need to cry you can. If you need to yell or lash out, I can bear it, she communicated to the child.

Eleanor attempted an awkward embrace, and the child collapsed against the spider's body, sobbing uncontrollably.

Eleanor hugged the child as best she could.

It will be OK. I am here for you. I will be your friend, and I will always protect you.

V

Shattered Alliances
Niwltir, +637 ER

Calder, the old gray-haired dwarf, sat down on a large rock several yards from a wall of mist that rose into the sky to meet the dark gray clouds covering the land. The rock was solid and stable on the hard ground beneath, and it fit firmly into the tree that had grown around it. He could sit on this rock with his back to the tree, keeping one eye on the mist and the other on rolling forested hills to the west. The sprawling land between the forest and the mist wall was covered with dirt and rocks.

He looked up and watched the setting sun illuminate the contours of the hills. Though he couldn't see the forested hills from where he sat, he knew they gave way to a land of hills and streams that had been cultivated into farmland by the hill dwarves. Calder reached into his pack, pulled out a stale chunk of bread, and sighed as he looked at it. He missed the fruit from the trees and the berries from the vineyards. Ever since the goblins had arrived, the hill dwarves found themselves losing farmland at an alarming rate. To see the devastation afterward, the trampled crops, the charred and barren trees, one would think the goblins thrived on destruction in and of itself. No one ever saw them looting or eating what the dwarves had so lovingly cultivated, but Calder reasoned that this was merely a chance lack of observation.

Calder pulled his cloak tighter around him and glanced over at the mist wall. He knew this was where he was supposed to wait for the mist walkers, but he was always uneasy around the wall. An expedition had once set out into the mist to explore, only to have one lone survivor come running back babbling about creatures of pure darkness with glowing eyes and endless appetites.

He shook his head to clear away the mental images that were giving strength to his fear and took a bite from the stale loaf.

The distraction worked. Calder was one of the dwarves of the forest, more prone to wandering than his hill dwarf cousins. He was one of the few that had spent many years developing the mental abilities that allowed him to communicate with the mist walkers, even though they were far away. The hill dwarves did not like being near the mist wall, so not only was it his job to play messenger, but he was also responsible for sitting and waiting in the cold for the elves to show up.

Calder looked around to make sure that everything was clear and then closed his eyes and reached out with his mind.

Where are you? The sun is setting, and travel will be much less safe the darker it gets.

Nothing.

Calder sighed and hopped off the rock, preferring to be already on his feet and ready to move if anything were to attack. He began to pace back and forth along the hard-packed earth. The dwarf turned to look out across the clearing toward the edge of the forest. He couldn't see any signs of movement and hoped it stayed that way.

A gentle breeze grazed the back of his mind, and he spun around to face the mist. Out strode three tall figures dressed in chainmail. The first elf was a male whose face showed lines of sorrow, yet whose expression was friendly. His hair was white and roughly shoulder length, tucked behind his pointed ears. His clothes were various shades of gray and white, his demeanor that of a scholar more than a warrior.

The second was a female with long dark hair tied back in a braid. She wore greens and browns over her chain mail, carried her bow at the ready, and constantly turned her head and eyes to take in everything around her. While the first had his focus on the dwarf, Calder could tell that the second had her attention on everything else.

The third and last figure seemed to be the youngest, though it was sometimes hard to tell with elves. He was dressed entirely in black with a shirt of mail under his black surcoat. The handles of two short swords protruded over his shoulders. His hair was black, nearly shoulder length, and he walked with his head somewhat bowed, as if he was depressed or bored.

The lead elf knelt in front of Calder so that they could more closely look each other in the eye. He then greeted Calder in the Dwarfish language; "Thank you for waiting, my friend. I am Bwriad, the female is Aderyn, and the young one is Talfryn."

Calder smiled and bowed to the elf. "It was no trouble. Now let us be on our way to the fortress."

Calder led the three elves through the forest on their way to the fortress. To aid in their stealth, he communicated silently to his guests as they went, so as to best bring them up to speed.

Three hundred and fifty-four years ago, the dwarves traveled through a sphinx gate deep in the mountains and began to settle this land. The mountain dwarves stayed in the northern mountain ranges, the hill dwarves cultivated the rolling hills to the south, and the forest dwarves mostly disappeared into the forests south of the hills. The forest dwarves discovered another sphinx gate to the far south. Ten years ago, the goblin hordes swarmed through and destroyed the gate guardians. Since then, they've been pushing us north toward the mountains.

The winter has iced over the passes in the mountains, and soon we shall be crushed against the frozen rocks.

*   *   *

When they arrived at the fortress a few days later, they were brought before the dwarf lord in charge of the land. His unpleasant disposition was etched in every line of his face as Calder led the elves before him. Styri, the dwarf lord, sat on a throne at the far end of the wooden great hall. On either side sat his chief advisers, equally distrusting and unsatisfied, though not as old as their liege.

"Do the elves think us so weak that only three of them can accomplish what hundreds of dwarves have failed to do?" asked Kol, the black-haired dwarf on the lord's right, as he tugged at his beard.

"Perhaps the elves merely don't care enough about our survival to send more than three of themselves," suggested Ildhar, the red-haired dwarf on the lord's left, as he gently stroked his beard.

Calder's gray brows furrowed in irritation. He stepped forward to speak to the dwarf lord but was interrupted.

"My esteemed dwarves," said Bwriad as he knelt and bowed before them. "We elves are not the most prolific of species and have grown accustomed to accomplishing much with as few as possible. We are here to aid your efforts, not to replace or overshadow them."

Styri snorted and stroked his beard that was black streaked with gray. "Welcome o' ageless wanderers. Make yourselves at home this night, for tomorrow you march to survey the enemy."

99

*　　　*　　　*

The next day, Calder rose early before the sun, only to find the elves standing outside waiting for him.

The four made their way through the mostly deserted fields and into the forest beyond. Calder picked up a trail and began tracking what was, most likely, a goblin patrol. He noticed that the female elf seemed to be tracing the trail farther off into the distance than his old eyes could see, but she kept quiet. The old dwarf grunted and kept going. It was most likely her way of showing him respect and not trying to overshadow him, but he still felt pangs of jealousy at his own limitations.

After some time, they crept up a small rise, keeping themselves low to the ground. As they peered around the trees and over the edge, they saw the goblin camp. The creatures were a little taller than dwarves with thinner, faster bodies that were mostly dark green splotched with shades of dark red. Goblins tended to travel in small groups of about fifty to a hundred so that they could easily raid the dwellings of their enemies and disappear again into the night. On their own, they rarely fought in large armies unless accompanied by much larger or more foul creatures. This particular group lacked any of these unwelcome additions, which gave Calder at least some small reason to be thankful.

The four carefully backed away from the edge and huddled together.

We can go back to the fort and get reinforcements, suggested Calder silently.

That will take too long and runs the risk of them moving or catching us on the way back. Let me do it. I can kill them all, returned the black-clad elf, for the first time uttering any words and showing a strange intensity as he did so.

100

What's with this "I" nonsense? Questioned Calder. *You can't kill 50 goblins by yourself. Those that don't kill you will escape, and the advantage of surprise will be lost.*

The older male elf looked at the female who nodded, then he turned back to Calder and readied his bow. *Aderyn will release the young one, and we will pick off any who try to escape. Stay hidden and bring word to your people should we fall.*

We won't, commented the young elf who took a stance, crouched on all fours, ready to climb back up the ridge and pounce like a hungry cat.

Calder shook his head in amazement and irritation. These damn elves were far too full of themselves, but before he could protest, he heard a sharp command from the female and instantly the young one was gone.

The other two elves took positions quickly on the top of the ridge and began turning this way and that, firing arrows at enemies Calder could not see.

Shamed by their foolish bravery, Calder climbed back up as quickly as he could and stopped dead in his tracks when he reached the top.

The young elf had caught most of the goblins by surprise, and some could still be seen rubbing the sleep from their eyes as they stumbled from their tents. The black-clad elf had drawn his two short swords and was quickly and gracefully cutting down every goblin he came across. As the goblins began to rush him, his twin swords lit up with blue flame and he moved quicker than before. Any who tried to flee were shot down by Bwriad and Aderyn. None could get behind the young elf as he twisted and spun through the camp, constantly changing direction in time to avoid a strike or behead an enemy.

Calder watched in amazement as the goblin camp was

destroyed. When the last goblin was slain, the young elf turned to look back at the three of them, his hair disheveled and sweat on his brow, but a smile across his lips.

The old elf sat down on the ground with a sigh and a pained expression.

"I think we owe you an explanation," said Bwriad as an astounded Calder looked at him. "This is Talfryn, First of the Dark Elves, and one of the living weapons of the Elvish Alliance."

*   *   *

Calder wiped the sweat from his brow as he stopped shoveling to enjoy the breeze as it swept across the fourth in a series of trenches they were digging around the fort. Upon advice from the elves, the dwarves had modified their fort into a star-like pattern, so sections of the walls could more easily defend the territory in front of other walls. This outer wall was then ringed by ditches in which were spikes, caltrops, and bear traps.

The white-haired male elf gained some respect among the dwarves when he rolled up his sleeves and began helping them build the walls and dig the ditches. The dwarf lord and his counselors oversaw the projects and were not so fond of the goodwill that their people showed the older elf.

Even more to his credit, the elf seemed to prefer the construction projects to the battles. The few skirmishes Calder had observed Bwriad in revealed a deep sadness and pain each time he killed. It stood in stark contrast to the sadistic grin of pleasure the young one had when he destroyed.

Calder had asked Bwriad about this at one point.

"I am old enough to remember a time before the wars and deaths. I have seen far too many of my people slain."

"What about the huntress who guards your backs?" Calder asked.

"She is a wood elf, while I am a high elf. I'm not sure if she's old enough to remember the times before our exile, but even so, the wood elves were always more predatory than we were, so it likely doesn't faze them as much."

"And what of the young one?"

"He is the first dark elf"; Bwriad sighed. "A product of the endless death that seems to surround us now. He has an incredible natural talent for killing and enjoys that more than any sentient being should. His dark gift made him an excellent choice to become the Council's weapon."

Calder paused, considering the politeness of his next question, "You say, 'first'. Does that mean there are more dark elves?"

"Yes. They are a common occurrence these days among our progeny. They have been instrumental in our endeavors against the Enemy. Since Cyfeiriad returned and the outer alliances were formed, they have been deployed to fight on many fronts."

Calder had pondered this over the past few days as they worked tirelessly on the construction projects. He wondered at the wisdom of using one's descendants to fight the battles you no longer had the stomach for. Mostly, he wondered what feeding that darkness inside the young one would do to him one day. Though outright murder and assault were rare among the dwarves, Calder had lived long enough to see jealousy, rage, or hatred twist someone's heart to murderous intent. He shook his head at the thought and returned to digging.

The female elf and the dark one had led a small group of dwarves into the forests to track, distract, or eliminate any goblin raiding parties until the preparations were complete.

The end goal of these projects was to lead a raid against the horde that surrounded the remains of the sphinx gate, lead them back to the fortress, and keep them occupied while another, smaller group would slip in and destroy the gate for good. That was the only way to make sure the goblins stopped coming.

As night fell, Calder trudged wearily back to the great hall after finishing the last of the traps in the fourth trench and covering them with leaves.

A greeting of cheers rose behind him, and he turned to see the other dwarves welcoming the raiding party back for the night. The dark elf was still smiling and seemed to be chatting uncharacteristically with his dwarven companions.

After cleaning himself up, Calder joined the other dwarves in the great hall, sitting in a relatively quiet corner where he could observe without being bothered.

The high elf and the wood elf sat in their own corner, eating their food and keeping to themselves.

The dark elf sat with the other warriors who had returned with him and a crowd of eager ears waiting to hear tales of their battles, since they had been gone for a couple weeks at this point.

Dwarven revelry was frequently drunk and rough by some standards, the dwarves enjoying a friendly brawl from time to time. Calder had never seen an elf take part in either, but the dark elf seemed to enjoy the interruptions of his meal to grapple or fight his comrades.

His eyes shifted to Styri and his counselors, eating their food and eyeing the festivities surrounding the dark elf with jealous glares.

*   *   *

104

The next day Calder readied himself to go out with the diversion and infiltration groups, but he was stopped by the high elf.

"I would like to ask you to stay behind and help coordinate the battle," Bwriad requested, kneeling in front of the dwarf.

Calder grunted; "I'm not so old that I can't fight."

"That is not the issue. If you allow me, I can further open your mind so that you are connected to all three of us and can monitor and convey the situation among us. During the battles we will not have the time or concentration to communicate remotely. Do you accept?"

The dwarf kicked the dirt and grumbled under his breath. He did not want to be left behind, but refusing would be a shameful sign of his own insecurities. "Fine."

"I will send my counselors, and you can link their minds to mine," declared the dwarf lord, walking up to the two of them.

They turned to look at Styri, dressed in the finest, most ornately decorated armor Calder had seen among his people. The armor, unlike that of most of the other dwarves, was without scratch, dent, or hint of dirt.

"Friend, Calder has had extensive training that makes him much more suited for this than you, though I am sure, with the proper training, you would be able to attain such skill," interjected Bwriad.

The corner of the dwarf lord's nostrils flared slightly, but he relented. "Very well. I shall send them as my emissaries in each party so that our soldiers are not without leadership, should the unthinkable happen on their missions."

Bwriad bowed his head to the dwarf lord. "Thank you for your understanding and generosity." He turned back to Calder. "Are you ready?"

The dwarf nodded.

The high elf swiftly grabbed Calder by the top of the head, squeezed his fingers, and closed his eyes. The dwarf's mind erupted into a chaos of visions: the view from the top of the walls looking down on the ground, a group of dwarves readying to leave through the main gate, and an agonized old dwarf collapsing to his knees.

Slowly the pain subsided and his vision returned to the world before him. The high elf opened his eyes and released him.

"Stay away from the main fight so you can concentrate," Bwriad instructed. If any of our missions fail, let the dwarf lord know so the plans can be modified."

Calder mumbled while rubbing his head and wandered off to find a place to sit down. He could feel Styri's gaze on his back and the gentle breeze moving around him.

*　　*　　*

Calder alternated between watching through the eyes of the wood elf and the high elf as they led their respective missions.

Aderyn led a group of dwarves in a straight-forward march to the broken sphinx gate, while Bwriad led another group in a wide arch to arrive at the East side of the gate. Both groups rode ponies to quicken their pace, though they did not push them hard so that they'd have strength and speed left over for the next part of the plan.

Their journeys were uneventful, yet Calder couldn't help but feel the adrenaline begin to pump through him the closer they got. If they were attacked or spotted before they reached their targets, then the whole plan would collapse.

Aderyn and her team reached their destination and hid

behind the trees having left their ponies several hundred yards behind. She looked out into the distance, and Calder saw the ruins of the gate surrounded by the camp of the enemy. A few patrols could be seen standing idly here and there.

His vision shifted to Bwriad taking a similar position on foot with his team far to the East and even farther from the camp.

*   *   *

Calder watched as Aderyn stepped from behind a tree, notched her first arrow, and released in one smooth motion. A goblin lookout dropped dead. She turned and repeated this process three more times, eliminating the closest lookouts before turning and motioning to the dwarves to follow her.

They approached the enemy camp, and Calder could see in amazing clarity the goblins, trolls, and wyverns milling about the camp in a large clearing that had been cut and smashed out of the surrounding forest. The green and red goblins patrolled the camp. The wyverns, dragon-like creatures with two wings, two hind limbs, and a tail, appeared to be grazing on a recent kill. The large, misshapen trolls mostly sat in tents or under awnings, lest the thick haze of clouds overhead should part and the sun turn them to stone. Calder hadn't realized how strong this group was, but he sensed no surprise from the wood elf.

She fired ten swift shots into the camp, dropping ten goblins in swift succession. A roar arose amid the enemy, and the trolls, goblins, and wyverns turned their attention toward the group, rushing forward to destroy them.

The dwarves readied small crossbows and fired once the first goblins were in range. The wood elf took several carefully aimed shots, blinding the first two trolls and a

107

wyvern. The enemy was then split between those having to deal with their blind, flailing companions, and those still running for their weapons and armor.

Aderyn and her group took advantage of this and retreated. They stopped just within sight of the nearest goblins and reloaded their crossbows, preparing to fight again. The goblins slowed as they approached crossbow bolt range and sent the trolls and wyverns ahead of them.

The trees were too close together for the wyverns to take to the air, but they were still dangerous on the ground. Aderyn raised her bow quickly to blind the nearest ones when a large object crashed through the branches overhead. She barely dodged a wyvern that had dived straight through the branches and into the ground.

Dwarves were knocked aside as the creature flailed its wings and tail. They righted themselves as quickly as they could and fired their crossbow bolts into the creature. The nearest dwarves rushed forward and finished it off with their axes and war hammers.

Calder saw the elf's vision spin back toward a rushing sound to see goblins starting to run at them as soon as the crossbows had been released. The elf shouted a command, and the dwarves took off as fast as they could. She stood her ground and began picking off as many goblins as she could before they got too close. At the last moment possible, she turned and ran.

The wood elf and her companions continued running, stopping only to shoot arrows or throw hatchets at their pursuers. The distance between them quickly diminished as the dwarves could not run as fast their enemies. They barely managed to make it to the ponies they'd left tied along the path. Once mounted, they were able to pick up speed and put more distance between them and the foul creatures.

Calder's attention slammed back into his immediate surroundings. "The decoy mission has been successful," he shouted up to the troops on the walls. The dark elf's head snapped up from staring at the ground, and he looked intently at the forest edge. The dwarf lord shouted orders and made his way up to the top of the wall.

*   *   *

Calder focused as the world around him faded into the edge of a wide clearing filled with abandoned tents and campfires surrounding the ruins of the shattered sphinx gate.

Bwriad led the dwarves quietly into the camp, his sword drawn and ready. They checked every tent as they went, though they only had to slay a handful of goblins. Everyone's head was on a swivel, their eyes darting from one shadow or corner to the next, waiting for as of yet unseen enemies to attack.

The center of the camp left a wide circle around the broken sphinx gate. Bwriad watched the dwarves reach out in wonder at the shattered gate guardians. They had been made of a kind of stone that contained a high concentration of various metals, giving them a unique hue and texture. He could make out just enough details from the broken stone to account for the four gryphons and three sphinxes that usually guarded the gate.

Calder had never seen the gate guardians shattered before, but he sensed concern and familiarity with the sight from the elf. It was said these apparent statues would come to life to prevent armies entering or leaving a gate.

Bwriad searched through the rubble until he found the shattered heads of the sphinxes. The blue crystal eyes were gone as were the red ones from the gryphons.

He made his way to the gate's main platform that stood as a large round disc composed of 15 concentric metal rings. Each ring was engraved with various symbols from a language that had yet to be identified. A disk about 6 feet across laid in the center of these 15 rings. The disc was an intricate metal lattice through which could be seen the hints of gears, gems, stones, lenses, and wires. Bwriad approached the central disc and looked up to see a bird alight on the other side.

Calder watched in amazement as the wisps of yellow-brown flame swirled around the bird, and it grew into the form of a man. The man's eyes were red-orange with yellow-brown flame-like swirls around the edge of the irises, creating an overall amber appearance. The man's hair was jet black. Calder did not recognize his accent or the clothes he wore.

"Those stupid creatures are too easily distracted, but I can't let you destroy this gate," the stranger said while stepping forward.

"Your presence answers the question of how mere goblins could have destroyed the gate so thoroughly," commented Bwriad.

"Their wish was my pleasure," said the amber-eyed man with a smile, holding out his hands as if gesturing to the world around him. "There's no problem we jinn can't solve." His eyes hardened and his brow furrowed; "They paid me handsomely to destroy the gate, but I'll kill you for free."

The amber-eyed jinn looked at the dwarves, who had all raised their crossbows toward him. He looked back at the elf. "More unwitting pawns?"

"They are not 'pawns.' The goblins attacked them first, and we came to their aid."

"Really?"

The jinn turned to the dwarves.

"You don't need to fight and die in their wars. They

suffer because they chose the wrong side, and all who join them suffer the same. My people were no different. Their 'enemy' will gladly welcome you."

"The Enemy was always a murderer, even from the beginning."

The jinn snorted.

"You're one to talk," he said, and a torrent of fire spewed from his outstretched hand.

Bwriad dived and rolled out of the way, shouting for the dwarves to stay back as he came to his feet.

Kol ordered the dwarves to fire, but their crossbow bolts were consumed by the jinn's yellow-brown flames that swirled around him as the missiles approached. Only then did he order the retreat.

The high elf stretched out his left hand, and an invisible force accelerated the air between him and the djinn. The airflow became a wind strong enough to dissipate the flames and long enough for him to leap at his opponent with his sword.

The jinn shifted into the form of a bird to dodge the attack, and began to fly upward. Bwriad reached up with his left hand, clenched his fist, and pulled downward. The bird slammed into the ground and shifted back into the form of a man. He reached out toward Bwriad, but the elf stepped on his hand and put his blade to the jinn's throat.

"Please surrender. I have no desire to slay you," he pleaded.

The jinn looked up with a smile; "I doubt that. I will never stop trying to kill your people for what they did to mine. And even if you kill me, you won't be able to stop the inevitable."

Bwriad heard a click and turned to see a device that had been hidden by the rubble. Its gears began to whir and the rings of the gate began to spin and lock into place. He slammed his sword straight down through the jinn's throat until it was firmly embedded in the earth. Not turning to see the results, he leaped toward the device, his hand outstretched to stop it, but it was too late. The last ring clicked into place, and the gate began to hum.

"Get as far away from here as you can and don't look back!" he shouted as he rushed to the center of the gate.

A small orb of swirling colors had begun to form in the center of the main disc. Bwriad quickly knelt down beside it and placed his right palm over the disc.

Calder's view of events turned black as Bwriad closed his eyes, though he was sure he saw a brief glimpse of white light shining out from under the elf's hand just before his eyes shut. A long moment passed, and Calder could see the silhouette of the elf's hand, though everything was tinted slightly red with very thin red lines. It took him a moment to realize that the light had become so bright that he was seeing the elf's hand through his eyelids. A moment later, everything went blindingly white. Calder closed his eyes and covered them with his hands reflexively before realizing that such efforts could not shield his mind's eye.

The light faded, and Calder could see the elf's vision attempt to return, but everything was faint and out of focus even though his eyes seemed to be open. He got the impression that the elf had collapsed onto his knees and had hunched forward. Several minutes passed before the sounds of dwarven footsteps reached the elf's ears.

"He destroyed the portal generator," said one dwarf in amazement.

"Turned it to slag," whispered another.

A set of footsteps approached closer than the others, and Calder could hear the voice of Kol to his left.

"The jinn claimed that your kind brought this war on them and you have this type of power, but you refused to use it," seethed the dwarf. "You risked our lives needlessly!"

"It's not like that," the elf struggled to say, weakly raising his torso and turning toward the dwarf who now came slightly more into focus. "The Enemy has twisted..."

"Enough of your elvish lies!" interrupted the dwarf. "We will not be your pawns any longer, nor will you get the chance to use this power against us."

A vague shadow shifted in the elf's vision, and Calder's connection shattered abruptly. He doubled over and vomited on the ground.

A horn blared, signaling the arrival of the decoy squad, and a guard rushed over to his side. "Were they able to get to the gate?"

Calder closed his eyes, trying to will the nausea away. "Yes, it is destroyed," he choked out before stumbling away from the walls to find a place to rest. Tears streamed down his face, while the vile urge to vomit at the back of his throat was mixed with the tightening of sorrow. He knew what had happened. He could hear the gates opening and the decoy squad returning, but he also knew that now was not the time. The elves would learn the truth, but first they must survive the battle.

Calder stumbled along until he found a small shed filled with hay for the ponies. He collapsed into the pile and let his mind drift into oblivion.

*   *   *

Calder's restless sleep was filled with images from the battle.

His vision rose swiftly up the steps to reach the wall,

focusing momentarily on the dark elf stationed there. Calder could see the wood elf reach the top of the wall, look at the dark elf, and say something in Elvish.

The dark elf's gaze shifted back to the forest edge as the goblins and trolls burst forth. He could hear the wood elf shouting orders for the dwarves to ready ballistas that had been set up on the inner corners of the spiked fortress walls. A moment later, wyverns stepped out of the tree line and took flight. There were only five left after the decoy's previous battle, and as they flew up, the ballistas fired.

Calder tossed and turned as he watched the large bolts soar through the air toward the wyverns that focused mostly on gaining altitude. Three were slain.

The two remaining wyverns swept in great arcs until they came at the ballistas from the sides while the dwarves struggled to reload and rotate them. Aderyn shouted for the dwarves to focus on the one coming from the East, while she and the young one took the one from the West.

The dark elf readied his own bow and waited for the wyvern to come into range. As soon as it did, he released, as did Aderyn. The arrows of both elves pierced the eyes of the wyvern. It flailed in the air in pain before losing its bearings and crashing inside the fortress. Calder's view turned to follow the winged beast's fall to the ground. The creature was soon set upon by dwarven soldiers piercing its sides with pikes.

Calder's sleeping body thrashed as he looked quickly to the far side of the fortress in time to see the other wyvern crashing into the ground outside the walls, its wings torn to shreds by the dwarves' crossbow bolts. The ballista had been reloaded and now fired down into the creature, impaling it to the ground.

Ignoring the screams of the dying monsters and the cheers of the dwarves, the dark elf turned back toward the approaching army. By now the goblins and the handful of trolls had discovered the spikes in the trenches surrounding the fort. Those who came second found a quick solution to the hazardous terrain: stomp their wounded allies into the ground so that their corpses could be used to safely bridge the gap, while the trolls leaped from one ridge to the next, or at least tried their best.

Orders were shouted and ballistas were aimed down toward the advancing trolls. Some shots were successful, but some missed. Two trolls made it between two spikes in the fortress wall's formation, placing them too close for the ballistas to hit them.

The dwarves surged along the walls and readied their crossbows. They fired and reloaded as quickly as they could, but the trolls rushed the inner meeting of the wall spikes. The great beasts grasped, tore, and beat at the wall. The dark elf rushed to the edge of the wall and stopped. He looked at the wood elf who shouted a command, and he leaped from the wall, drawing his swords in midair. As he descended toward the first troll, he flipped the blades so that they pointed down as if to stab, and then they burst into blue flame.

The burning blades sunk deep into the back and shoulders of the first troll. As it staggered backward and tried to reach for him, the dark elf shifted his weight to the left, freed the blade in his right hand, and sank it into the troll's skull. He barely managed to avoid being crushed as the lifeless creature fell backward to the ground.

The second troll reached into the gap they had made in the wall, pulled free a broken beam, and turned to swing it at the elf. As the makeshift cudgel swung toward him, the dark elf charged, dove forward, and rolled under the creature. He spun up and out of his roll, slashing the tendons across the back of the beast's ankles and knees. It began to wobble on unsteady legs.

The elf ran toward the wall, took a few running steps up its surface, and then pushed off, twisting in midair so that he again hooked his blades into the troll. The force of the impact knocked the troll forward. The troll tried to catch himself with his hands rather than reach for his attacker. As it fell, the dark elf freed his left blade and flipped it back into its normal blade-up position, bringing it to his right shoulder. When the creature's hands hit the ground, the elf swung his blade in an arc and severed the creature's head.

The dark elf rose from the corpse and looked up to see the goblin lines being slowed slightly by a rain of bolts and arrows. Calder's eyes darted beneath his closed lids as he watched the line getting closer. He could see that the time it took to reload allowed those who survived to trample their fallen in order to get closer to their prey.

The dark elf rushed forward to meet the first of the goblins to approach the gap. Calder wondered if it was a strategy to keep them away from the breach as long as possible, or if it was merely the young elf's desire to kill that motivated him.

The elf sliced and turned, twisted and spun, stabbed and cut as the goblins kept charging. A few moments later, a shout arose behind him, and the sound of heavily armored dwarves could be heard running up to aid him, having been inspired by his bravery.

Calder lost track of how many the dark elf killed or even which way he was facing in regard to the lay of the land. All he saw was enemy after enemy, cut and pierced by the blue flames surrounding the elf's blades.

The chaos stopped and the elf came to a sudden halt as a hand grasped his shoulder and the wood elf's voice uttered an Elvish command. He seemed to stagger slightly, as if the momentum of his body and mind had been so caught up in the battle that he was unable to stop their forward movement.

The dwarves cheered as the remaining enemies scattered. They were diminished greatly with no way of gaining reinforcements through the sphinx gate.

Calder shifted unpleasantly in his sleep, and his vision shifted to that of the wood elf as she made her way back into the fortress. The dwarf lord stopped her and asked about the burning blades and how such things could be crafted.

"The flames cannot be separated from the wielder," was her only reply before continuing on.

The battle over and the dwarven settlement relatively safe, Calder finally felt himself relax and release his grip on the elves' minds.

*　　　*　　　*

Darkness greeted Calder's eyes as they opened slowly. His head and stomach felt better, but his joints were now stiff and sore from laying awkwardly in the pile of hay for so long. With a grimace and a groan, he heaved himself to his feet and rubbed his neck. He made his way back to the great hall with a somewhat unsteady gate as his stiff joints reluctantly allowed him to move.

He wandered through the kitchens and into the great hall via the side entrance.

Huddled near the throne were the dwarf lord and his two counselors. They were examining something between them.

"Are you sure they won't wake up?" said the black-bearded one.

"I told you, they'll be out for days. The poison induces an almost deathlike sleep from which they can only be

117

awakened by the antidote," replied Ildhar.

The dwarf lord examined something in his hands. "We may not be able to obtain the secret of Bwriad's power, but we can at least obtain the secret behind these blades." He stretched out his arm and made several slashes and stabs with a familiar-looking short sword. The blades remained as plain, well-crafted steel without a trace of blue flame.

"What did you do?" asked Calder as he stepped into the light.

The three dwarves turned to look at him with surprise that quickly turned to glares.

"We must not be dependent on or trust the elves," said Ildhar.

"They use us as pawns in their great wars," said Kol.

"We shall either decipher their secrets or pry them out," declared the dwarf lord, as he closely examined the swords for markings or mechanisms. He turned to his counselors. "Even as they sleep, I want them bound and taken to the dungeon. We will start with the young one first. Take only the most loyal guards with you. The young one seems especially to have bewitched many of our kin."

The two counselors bowed to their lord.

A loud bang drew all attention to the doors of the great hall as one of the dwarf guards came flying through. The now open doorway was quickly darkened by the figure of the dark elf as he strode toward the three. Calder stepped back to separate himself from them.

The dark elf carried the dwarf guard's axe in his right hand. He clenched his fist around the wooden handle, and the whole axe burst into blue flame. The shadows in the great hall lengthened and deepened as the elf continued forward.

Kol stepped forward and began to draw his own axe to fight. The elf threw his and embedded it into the counselor's skull.

Ildhar stepped forward, but the elf was on him before he could draw his weapon. One hand stopped the dwarf from pulling his war hammer free, while the other latched tight on his throat and began to pierce between the tendons to crush the windpipe. Calder could see a strange mix of rage and pleasure in the elf's expression.

A commanding voice gave the young elf pause. Calder turned to see the wood elf standing in the doorway.

The dark elf turned his head, without releasing his prey, and shouted something back in Elvish to the female. She replied and he released the nearly dead dwarf, who fell to the ground with a thud.

"Return what you have stolen," ordered the wood elf to the dwarf lord.

"How dare you come into my hall and give me orders!" roared the dwarf, gripping both swords as if he might use them himself.

"If you return what you stole, we will leave without incident and never return. There will not be any further retribution for your betrayal... or for your murder of a high elf."

The dark elf glared at the dwarf lord with murderous intent, and the dwarf glared back in proud defiance.

"I saw what your counselor did to the high elf," said Calder, stepping forward. "Your people murdered one of theirs and poisoned the others to steal from them. We can't afford more enemies."

The dwarf lord turned his ire on Calder; "You have no right to tell me what to do. I am lord of this hall and of these lands. My authority is absolute, and no one, not some damned elf or self-important forest trash, will defy me!"

Calder's anger rose within him and he stepped forward,

slamming his foot into the cold earth and bellowing as he did, "Enough!"

The ground beneath the dwarf lord shook and he fell to his knees with a gasp as his eyes widened. Calder took advantage of his shock to relieve him of the swords.

He returned them to the dark elf, bowing his head and uttering an apology as he did so.

The wood elf thanked him, and the two elves turned and left in silence.

Once they were both gone from the great hall, Calder turned to the fallen dwarf lord. There were ways to rightfully depose him within their culture, but Calder did not look forward to it. He was getting too old for this.

The old dwarf approached the dwarf lord, reached out, grabbed him by the hair, and dragged him from the great hall. The dwarf lord tried to struggle, but Calder was firmly rooted to the earth with each step he took. He hoped his people would understand and that the dwarves as a whole would not suffer for the mistakes of a few.

VI

At First Sight
Dynoltir, +2003 TR

A man of indeterminate age and stern eyes sat in a barren room surrounded by cinderblock walls. A table and two chairs had been placed in the middle of the room, with one of the chairs occupied by a kind older woman in her early sixties.

The man with stern eyes pulled a recorder from his pocket and set it on the table. He pressed one of the buttons.

"Please state your name and occupation for the record."

"My name is Elizabeth Hanover. I am a psychic investigator, though I would consider it more of a vocation than an occupation," replied the woman with a smile.

"Very well. Please relate to us the events as best you can."

"It started on a Tuesday..."

*   *   *

I was eating dinner alone in my home when I got the call. The man on the other end asked me if I really was able to communicate with spirits. I informed him that yes, I was. He was like so many that I hear from: somewhat nervous and skeptical. He introduced himself as Scott Trevor and explained that he wanted me to investigate the haunting of his home.

We arranged a meeting a few days later at his house, which was built in the older section of town, probably in the early 20th century. I didn't sense anything when I first arrived, which isn't that unusual. Frequently, spirits will hide themselves until pushed. The house itself was large and old.

When Scott opened the door and I saw that he was only in his mid to late 20's, I wondered how he could afford such a place. When I stepped inside, it all made sense.

I could feel the presence immediately. Whatever was inhabiting the house was old and very bitter. It did not like living people. My guess would be that very few had stayed in the house for long, so the price was much lower than it would have been otherwise.

Scott led me to the dining room, where he began to explain what he had experienced. When he first moved into the house, nothing seemed amiss. It was always slightly cool and had the usual creaking noises of an older home but nothing more. After a few weeks, he began hearing footsteps. He'd get up and check the whole house, but everything was locked, and no one was in the house. It unsettled him at first, but he eventually learned to sleep through the night.

A couple nights later, the footsteps were accompanied by the sounds of claws scraping along the walls. He would search the house, hear a noise or see movement out of the corner of his eyes, but when he'd turn, nothing was there. Night after night, this kept happening, which started making him paranoid. Every night he'd lock himself in his room and barricade the door, just to get some sleep. He tried the police, but they never found anything. Even with the door locked and barred, he'd still hear the steps and scratching on the other side. The first night he managed to fall asleep, soon after the noises started, they moved into the room.

This time there was a growl. He tried his bedside lamp, but the bulb burst. He could hear it pacing in his room. Scott left his room and barricaded himself in another. No matter which room he tried to seek shelter in, the noises followed. He could only sleep during the day, and even then, only for a few hours.

Weeks of this went by before the next escalation. Scott was exhausted to the point that he just collapsed on the floor. He awoke sometime later to the sounds of claws raking the floorboards near his head and a deep menacing growl right at his ear. He could feel the breath on his neck.

Scott snapped awake and scrambled away. That's when he saw it for the first time, on all fours like an animal, limbs out at odd angles. The hair was long and ragged, the fingers ended in claws, not nails. It raised its head and rushed at him. The creature's body was female. Its face was sunken and wasted, as if half starved. The creature opened its mouth, the flesh at the corners tearing open so that its jaws could open beyond human capacity. Its mouth was filled with long, sharp teeth. The creature roared in his face and then stopped.

Its brows furrowed in anger and then it just vanished.

Scott had not seen or heard the creature since. I must admit, this definitely sounded strange. The entity had wanted to torment him, but then it just stopped? Scott said that since that night, he hadn't seen or heard anything unusual in the house at all. The entity must have been hiding itself from him, since I could still sense its malevolence and frustration all around us.

Scott was eager to learn more about the entity. He wanted to know how it came to be in his home, where it came from, who it was, and what it wanted. I was glad he hadn't let the experience taint him with too much negativity, but something still seemed slightly off. I agreed to come back the next night and attempt to communicate with the entity.

The next night I arrived just after sunset. The night was pleasantly cool, and I walked into the house with an optimistic sense of the situation. Since most of the events had taken place in his bedroom, we set up in there.

We sat on the floor holding hands in the middle of his

room. I closed my eyes and reached out with my mind to contact the entity. It did not respond immediately, but I could feel its presence.

I told Scott that I could feel it and asked him to give me some questions. His first was to know its name. After a little coaxing, the entity revealed that it was named Irene. From then on, I called it by name.

Scott next wanted to know where it was from. Irene refused to answer, so he asked how it came to be in the house. Irene said it was hers. When he asked what it wanted, the answer was accompanied by a wave of anger and frustration. Irene wanted him to leave. Scott calmly refused, stating that it was his house. Immediately after, I could feel a chill on my neck as it whispered in my mind, *tell him to get. Out. Of. My. House.*

"Why does he need to leave?"

I hate him and everything about him. This is my home, and he should leave.

Scott again stated that he refused to leave his house. He was remarkably calm and composed the whole time. None of this helped though. The entity began to claw at the floorboards around us and growl from the shadows.

I then asked it, "What binds you to this house?" I thought that maybe if we could release the entity, then it could be at peace. I immediately regretted it.

Irene grabbed me from behind and threw me across the room. My body hit the wall hard. Before I could recover, I could feel her claws digging into me again and lifting me off the floor. My face felt cold as she whispered in my mind.

There's a necklace behind a loose brick in the back of the fireplace. Take it. Take that necklace out of here, and I can leave!

"Why are you so intent on avoiding him," I asked.

There was no reply.

Irene lowered me to the ground, and I then lost track of its presence. Scott helped me up, and I said I should probably go for the night.

When we got downstairs, I asked him for some water. While he went to get it, I searched the back of the fireplace for the loose brick. Just behind it was a small alcove with a locket on a small silver chain. Inside the locket was a small stone. Blood covered the inside and outside of the locket, holding the stone in place.

Scott returned and asked what I'd found. I showed him and explained that if I took it, the entity might leave and he would have peace and quiet. He said he appreciated the sentiment, but that he'd hold onto the necklace for now so that he could try to learn more about Irene. It was his house and his decision, so I let him. We said our goodbyes and made plans for him to call me if he needed further assistance.

That was the last I heard from him, more than six months ago by now.

* * *

The man with the stern eyes sat in the same room across from an apparently empty chair. A locket sat on the table a few inches from the recorder.

"Let the record show that the interviewee refuses to appear or sit in the chair. Please state your name out loud for the record."

"I am Irene Thomas," came a disembodied voice.

"Tell me how this all started."

A growl rumbled out of the empty air in front of him as the chair rose quickly and crashed into the wall.

"Just let the void take me."

125

"I will decide who the void takes. Now, tell me how this started," he said with fading patience.

Another growl echoed in the cement room.

"Fine."

*   *   *

I was born in the early 1920s. I was not the healthiest of children, too weak to play or do much else other than lie in bed, and my parents quickly exhausted all scientific and medical options at their disposal.

That's when they turned to the occult.

My parents had been casually fascinated with psychics, mysticism, and magic, but when their only daughter only got weaker and science failed them, they became obsessed. We traveled as a family around the world, or sometimes one of my parents would go alone. They interviewed every psychic, witch, or shaman they could find. If there was a rare ancient text that might apply, they bought it. I remember my mother being worried some nights about the dark allies my father was visiting in order to acquire books and scrolls through the black market.

Eventually they must have found something. I don't know what it was exactly, but they started injecting me with it soon afterward. And it worked.

Within days, I was stronger and healthier than I'd ever been. My parents were ecstatic that I could finally run and play with other children.

But their joy was short lived.

My form had always been thin and frail, but after the injections, it didn't matter. I was stronger and faster than any of the other kids at school. After a few weeks though, my appearance began to change. My face became sunken and

126

deathly pale. I wasn't any weaker, but I looked like I was starved and about to die. I could hear my parents arguing at night sometimes.

A little while later, the thirst kicked in. I was constantly thirsty, but for what I did not know. No drink that we had in our home would satiate me. I began to see the life and vitality in the people around me.

I hated it.

And I craved it.

My parents started getting complaints about me from the school. I was becoming increasingly cruel to my classmates. It started off small with verbal jabs at people's insecurities, but then it escalated. In less than a month I was kicked out for delightedly breaking several bones in one kid's body and licking the tears off his face while he cried.

After that, my parents kept me at home.

I quickly grew restless. Eventually I tortured and killed all of our pets. When they were gone, I started catching rats in the basement and torturing and killing them too.

My parents became more worried about me. When I was caught sneaking out and forced to confess that I was the reason the neighborhood pets had disappeared and that random people were found in alleys with several bones broken, they decided to lock me up in the basement.

I spent the next decade of my life down there. Periodically my parents would release various small animals for me to torment, kill, and feed on. Sometimes, my mother would even try to tell me stories. I didn't much care about the stories.

My parents had had me late in life, so by the time I was in my early twenties, their bodies had started to decline. It made tripping my father down the stairs, subduing him, torturing him, and feeding on him quite an easy task. I think this is what finally gave my mother the strength and resolve to do it.

A few days later, my mother left the basement door open at night. I crawled up the stairs on all fours as was my nature by that time. I made it halfway down the carpeted hall before I stepped in the bear traps. She had replaced the usual long, thick rug with a thinner one and placed traps underneath. My right wrist got caught first. I howled in pain and fell to my left, setting off another that grabbed my left thigh. As I collapsed to the ground, my left arm reached out and landed in a third trap. Before I could do anything to free myself, I heard my mother rush down the hall and impale me against the wall with a spear through my right shoulder. The last thing I remember was glaring at her and trying to pull myself along the spear, and then she decapitated me.

I think it was several decades later before my mind finally reassembled itself enough for me to be aware of what had happened. I no longer had a physical body, but I could move things. My hatred for the living grew even more. I soon learned that I could feed on people's fear, panic, or anxiety. Their suffering was my sustenance. And so I haunted and tortured every poor soul that moved into that house.

*   *   *

"Where does the locket come from?" asked the main with the stern eyes.

"It was a gift from my parents when I was young. I still had it around my neck when my mother decapitated me. It's infused with my blood from my death."

"Now tell me about your experiences once Scott moved in."

"At first it was just the usual. He responded the way

everyone did. His fear and distress were delicious. Everything was going great until the night I revealed myself. That's when his fear disappeared."

*   *   *

When I reveal myself, people either run away, their mind breaks, or they become my hapless victim until they eventually starve to death. But this was different. The way he looked at me wasn't right. His fear was gone, and his mind wasn't shattered.

The next night it got stranger. He started talking out loud to me. Like he was trying to start a conversation. Mediums and psychics would sometimes try to talk to me, but that was different. They wanted to know what I wanted so that they could get rid of me or end the torment of their clients. It never worked. The things he said... they left me feeling uncomfortable.

No one had ever reacted this way. I became more and more frustrated. He would come back every night and start asking about the people who used to live there, trying to figure out which one I was.

The most disturbing part was, I think he wanted to spend time with me. He'd just sit there and talk about his day sometimes. He'd ask me questions about myself, but not in fear or academic curiosity. It was as if he wanted to get to know me.

I was disgusted. This perverse behavior from him made me sick. When the psychic asked what kept me there, a way to escape leaped into my mind. Maybe if she took the locket, I could go with her. I could be free of this perverse freak and go back to feeding on people like I used to.

129

*   *   *

The air around him roared with another unearthly growl as the table in front of him was cracked with a loud crash by unseen hands.

"But that freak wouldn't let me leave!"

"Let the record show that Irene has broken the table," he said, glaring at the empty air before him and leaning his elbows on the table.

"That's why I agreed to this. You can free me from this disgusting human. Let the void take me."

"Are you sure that's what you really want? Once you are taken, there is no going back."

He waited in silence several minutes for an answer that never came.

*   *   *

A young man in his late twenties now sat in the seat across from the man with the stern eyes.

"State your name for the record."

"My name is Scott Trevor."

Scott reached out and ran a finger over the crack in the table. He looked back at his interviewer.

"Tell me what happened."

"Well, I think the psychic already told you everything. When I first moved in it started small with the noises, and then it just kept getting worse. Constantly sleep deprived, scared, and stressed, I was nearing the end of my sanity."

"What happened the night Irene revealed herself that changed everything?"

"What changed was that she did reveal herself. When I saw her for the first time, I was struck by the sight of her. She was the most beautiful creature I had ever seen. I knew from then on this was the one for me. I felt an immediate attraction to her. I had to get to know her.

"I tried talking to her. I'd tell her about myself and how my day had been. I event tried to research the history of the house to hopefully find out about her past. But none of it worked.

"That's why I contacted the psychic. It wasn't as helpful as I had hoped, since she didn't open up to the psychic any more than she had to me. But the locket taught me two things. The first was a clue that led me to figure out who Irene used to be, and the second was that she wanted to leave.

"I must admit that I was heartbroken at first. The sense of rejection was incredibly painful. Logically, I had tried my best to befriend her, but she hadn't reciprocated. If she didn't want to even be friends; it was her choice. But emotionally it still hurt."

*   *   *

"Why didn't you get rid of the locket?"

"I thought about it for a long time. At one point, the pain of rejection made me want to just throw it in the river, but then it passed. I tried to think about things dispassionately, so I wouldn't let my emotions cloud my judgment. I realized that I couldn't let her leave. Despite my attraction to her, she was still a creature that enjoyed tormenting people, and I couldn't just let her torment someone else."

"Did you read the transcript of her interview I sent you?"

"Yes. It made me rather sad, but I think I understand better now. Her parents loved her enough to search every dark corner of this world to find a cure for her. But they weren't strong enough to face her darkness or try to fix it. They just hid her away and let the darkness consume her. If they'd loved her more or been stronger, then they would have fought it. They wouldn't have let their daughter be consumed by it. I think that's also why she was so disgusted and said that I made her sick. Irene's been so full of hatred, rage, and bitterness all this time that to experience or sense anything kinder makes her sick and probably unpleasantly aware of the things she's done wrong. I can't condone her previous actions, but I can at least offer to help her find a better way. Maybe my friendship can help start her on a better path. I don't know..."

*   *   *

The man with the stern eyes stood alone in the room and turned back to the recorder.

"Final notes. Irene refused to comment after I let her listen to Scott's interview. She decided against the void. Since the last recording, the entity, known as Irene, and the human, Scott Trevor, have decided to both let each other exist in peace in the house. I have not fed Irene to the void; however, both have been warned. As long as she harms no one else, I will let her be. If she takes another life, I will be back, and the void will have her without hesitation."

He turned off the recorder and returned it to his pocket. The man left the room, made his way out of the nondescript building, and walked back to his car. The sun was rising as he wound his way through various neighborhoods before stopping in front of a particular house.

A girl with unkempt hair and a mischievous smile that combined to form the appearance of friendly craziness exited the front door of the house. She carefully and quietly shut the door before tiptoeing across the wooden porch. Once on the pavement, she dashed to the car and got inside.

The man's stern eyes softened, and he smiled at his daughter.

VII

Henry and Adelaide
Dynoltir, +1887 TR

Adelaide's mind drifted slowly upward, gradually becoming aware of the cold, damp air on her face and the warmth of the course blanket wrapped tightly around her. Focusing on the warmth, she began to drift back to sleep.

A harsh ringing buzz jarred her back to consciousness, and she reluctantly reached an arm into the cold air to shut off her clockwork harasser.

She flung back the blanket and sat up, the cold air rousing her to full wakefulness. Looking out the soot-covered window of her small, brick-walled, closet-like apartment, she could see the changing colors of the sky indicating the setting sun.

Adelaide checked the time on the clock and quickly readied herself for the night shift ahead of her. She put on the jumpsuit she had worn at the factory. Stained with oil and soot, it was made from thick, course fabric. While not the most pleasant of materials, it provided warmth and no small amount of protection from sharp objects.

She pulled back her hair and used a small strip of leather to tie it in place. While it might be more practical and safe in the factory to cut her hair like a boy or shave it off completely, she had decided to keep it at least shoulder length, so her teenage youth was not completely consumed and destroyed by the unfortunate necessities of survival. Her mother had never wanted her to work in the factories, but since her mother had vanished six months ago, there was no other choice.

Adelaide usually tried to keep her head down when she

walked through the narrow, cobbled streets between the tall brick buildings, but sometimes she couldn't help but look up longingly at the last rays of light as the sun finally set.

There wasn't much to see, unfortunately, as smoke from the factories tried to usurp the clouds for dominance of the sky. She barely caught the glint of light off of the gargoyles perched on the corners of the buildings overhead.

With a sigh, she lowered her head and continued on to the factory.

*   *   *

Adelaide clocked in for her shift at the factory, put on her protective goggles, and set about her daily tasks. It was mind-numbing work on an assembly line with the only natural light coming from small windows high up the walls near the ceiling. Most of the lighting came from the new electric lights strung overhead. She didn't know what she was helping to make, only that part A attached to part B after a fashion. Her mind fell into a haze so that she was less aware of the achingly slow progress of the hours.

By the time her shift ended, her skin was darkened with dirt wherever exposed, leaving only two circles around her eyes that were clear when she removed the goggles she wore to protect them. She also noticed that some days she coughed more than others by the end of her shift.

As she made her way outside, she looked up, trying to catch the first rays of light as the new day began. The sky was still murky with smoke, but as the light was growing, she could faintly see the outlines of the gargoyles all along the edges of the roof tops above her.

Fatigue and her tedium-dulled mind tilted Adelaide's head toward the ground as she trudged back home. Her mind was only just drifting out of its factory-induced haze, so it took her several minutes to realize that something wasn't right.

But by then it was too late.

Horrific screeches and rushing wind filled the air. Adelaide looked up to see the gargoyles falling from the roofs. No. Not falling, they were diving. They were diving toward the people on the street.

A great steal beast with fiery eyes and an eerie glow emanating from the cracks in its chest plates slammed into a pedestrian several feet ahead of her. It turned quickly and raked its claws through two more people, rending them asunder before the screams of bystanders alerted the entire street.

Now fully awake and alert, Adelaide ran for cover. She dashed into an alley that had been on her right and hid between several crates and a brick wall. Carefully, she peered through the gaps and watched in horror as the metal creatures tore into people and buildings, hunting down those who tried to hide.

A sudden sound caught her attention and she turned in fright, expecting to see one of the machines coming for her. Instead, she saw a young man. He was hiding on the other side of the alley, his movements jerking forward and back as if he was unsure whether he wanted to run forward or hide. He was in his late teens, and she recognized him from the factory. He was taller than her with a strong build, but not overly bulky. from loading and unloading crates every night. His appearance of strength made his uncertain, almost fearful movements seem strange.

What was he doing? Did he want to get himself killed? The idiot needed to hide, or he was going to die too.

The young man kept touching something under his shirt above his chest. He took one final step back, and then she saw his face change. He'd made up his mind. He reached into his shirt and pulled out a small dark rock fastened around his neck by a cord. He ripped it free and clenched his fist by his side. She could see blood dripping from his hand.

A strange light seeped from his fist. Matter and energy spiraled up his arm toward his back, and he began to fall forward. The light split directions from there, following the length of his spine downward and up until it reached the base of his skull. The matter and energy wrapped around his body from back to front as if consuming the young man. By the time his hands hit the ground, they were no longer hands. What stood in the alley was a large, scaled creature, about six feet high at the shoulder with four legs, two wings, and a long tail. The boy had turned into a dragon. She gasped at the sight and instinctively stepped back against the brick wall.

The dragon's claws dug into the pavement, and it hurled itself into the street. Adelaide turned to watch through the cracks between the crates as the dragon tore into the metal gargoyles. Its claws rent, its fingers crushed, and its teeth shattered the gargoyles. The more he fought them, the more they came at him, until it seemed none were left terrorizing the street. The dragon twisted and coiled, evading and striking its way through the last swarm of metal creatures. Eventually, the light had gone out of all of them, and only mangled cooling lumps of metal remained.

With that, the dragon took to the air and disappeared into the smoke and clouds.

*   *   *

Henry shoved the last crate into the back of the truck as the nighttime signal for the mid-shift break blared across the factory. After retrieving his meal, he went outside to the yard to eat. The bright factory lights blocked his view of the stars, yet the cool night air felt refreshing.

He mused that even if the yard lights hadn't been so bright, he probably couldn't have seen the stars through the almost ever-present smoke and haze that lingered over the city. He sighed. Such was the price of progress, or so the newspapers said.

Henry unwrapped the bandage around his right hand and examined the cuts on his palm from the day before when the steel gargoyles attacked. They were already beginning to heal. It had hurt quite a bit to tear the stone back out of his palm afterward, but at least the monstrosities were destroyed. Henry rewrapped his hand, turned to look at the shadows beyond the borders of the factory fence, and his mind drifted off as he stared into the darkness at the edge of the yard.

"Do you mind if I join you?"

Henry's head snapped back to reality and toward the direction of the voice. A girl, maybe in her early to mid-teens, was sitting next to him and pulling out her lunch. He'd seen her around the factory before but didn't know her. So, why was she talking to him?

Henry shrugged in response to her question and started eating his sandwich as an excuse not to interact.

They sat and ate their respective meals in silence, much to Henry's relief.

"My name's Adelaide. What's yours?"

Henry reluctantly looked at the girl. He didn't want anyone's attention, but not responding would make things worse.

"Henry."

More silence passed and he hoped, perhaps, she had lost interest in the conversation.

"Did you see the strange gargoyle attack yesterday?"

He wasn't sure if he should be worried or not by the question, but he decided to answer anyway as the attack was hard for anyone to miss.

"I saw it mentioned in the papers, but there was no explanation of where it came from or why it happened."

"Yeah, when I asked the boss this morning about how it would affect things here, he only said to let him know if I was going to quit, so he could hire someone else to replace me."

Henry heard her sigh and glanced over to see her head drooping slightly.

Silence reinstated itself and Henry hoped it would be victorious this time.

"So how did you hurt your hand?"

A surge of fear swept through him at the question, but he swallowed, looked down at his bandaged hand, and said, "I cut it."

The signal marking the end of breaktime rang out, and Henry quickly departed back to work, relieved at the provided means of escape.

*   *   *

The next night, Adelaide made her way to where she'd found Henry the previous shift, but he wasn't there. She looked around frantically. There wasn't much time on their breaks for her to get to know him.

She walked back into the factory and checked the break room, but he wasn't there either. Moving as swiftly as she could without attracting attention, she moved through the factory to the loading docks.

Adelaide heaved a sigh when she found him sitting on one of the docks and eating his meal. Without further

139

hesitation, she made her way over to him and sat down to eat.

Out of the corner of her eye, she saw him turn and look at her while she unwrapped her sandwich. She wanted to know so bad how he had turned into a dragon and what he knew about the metal gargoyles, but she didn't want to scare him away. One of her first observations of him had been how quickly he disappeared at the end of his shift. She didn't know how he did it, but it made her realize that she would be better off trying to earn his trust rather than follow him after work to figure out what was going on.

"So, what do you like to do when you're not here?" she asked, hoping to spark some conversation from him.

He seemed to pause, and she watched his movements closely as he looked up at the sky and said, "Look at the stars."

She followed his gaze, unable to see anything through lights around the factory and the ever-present haze that lingered over the city.

"Do you know some place where you can see past the constant smoke?"

Henry didn't respond, so she went back to eating, trying to think of something to get him talking.

"What about your parents? What are they like? What do they do?"

"They're dead," he said plainly and took another bite of his meal.

A twinge of guilt poked her heart as she hung her head; "My father died in a factory explosion when I was little. My mom worked hard to take care me, but she disappeared about six months ago. At this point, I'm pretty sure she's dead too."

Out of the corner of her eye, she saw him turn toward her, a look of pain and sympathy in his eyes. She kept still, unsure of what would come next, but not wanting to ruin her chance.

"I'm sorry to hear that. My parents died a long time ago." He paused and looked down. "If you ever need or want help, just let me know."

Adelaide's eyes widened in surprise a moment before the signal blared to return to work. She turned just in time to see Henry hopping off the loading dock and walking away. Maybe this connection would help him open up.

*   *   *

Henry had grown to enjoy his daily conversations with Adelaide. Few at the factory knew anything about him, which was for the best. He couldn't trust anyone, which made his life somewhat lonely and hard at times. Making things worse was the fact that the factory was not the most enjoyable place. Having at least one person to talk to made it more bearable. The feeling was like something he hadn't felt in a long time and made him both happy and scared. He was thankful for the friendship and being able to relax a bit, but he was nervous that he might slip up and reveal more than he should.

Despite the lessening of his burden in some ways, he still felt drained by the end of the week. Pretending to be what he was not proved exhausting, especially with the increased interaction with Adelaide. He looked forward to disappearing from these people for even a couple days.

As soon as the final signal blasted across the factory, Henry was gone. He made his way as quickly as he could without drawing suspicion through the cobbled streets and alleys. The first few rays of the morning sun began to sneak past the smoke and haze overhead. Stepping into a particularly warm and bright ray of light that had somehow managed to creep between the tall brick walls, he stopped and closed his

141

eyes to enjoy the feeling of the sun on his skin. The warmth on his cold flesh was a pleasant change from the cold nights and mornings he was used to.

His thoughts were interrupted by shrieks and screams... again.

Henry turned to look back the way he had come in time to see one of the metal gargoyles shoot past the opening of the alley as it attacked a fleeing pedestrian.

He hesitated, his mental fatigue urging him to rest, while the memory of his own life being saved by someone else flashed through his mind. He couldn't just leave people to die, but he was so tired. The stone was cold against his chest beneath his shirt as he tapped his fingers on it in indecision.

The sound of bricks breaking and a scream cut short made the decision. Henry reached into his shirt and grabbed the stone. He clenched his fist and felt the cold sharp edges dig into him again. A tingle spiraled up his arm, and his body pitched forward. He could feel the energy reach his spine and spread up and down its length. The energy and matter stretched and reached around from his back to his front as if consuming him. His body continued to fall, and dragon's claws hit the ground.

Henry twisted and sprang up the side of the building next to him, leaping into the swarm of metal gargoyles attacking the city. Fighting and destroying the creatures was exhilarating yet stressful. The feeling of his mind and body twisting and coiling as he climbed the sheer brick walls to pounce down on the monsters in the street, or soared through the air to destroy them before they reached the crowds was nearly intoxicating. The fear of injury and the sight of torn human corpses that he hadn't saved in time filled him with dread and guilt.

Eventually, the battle ended, but not before one of the

gargoyles had managed to tear Henry's left wing, so he couldn't fly away and change back out of sight. He leaped down into a demolished building nearby that still had a mostly intact outer wall to try shielding his dragon form from view. With his left claws, he dug into his right scaly hand and tore out the stone, clenching his jaw and grinding his teeth in an effort to hold in a roar of pain. The dragon's body slumped slightly, as if all of its muscles relaxed at once. Then its flesh sloughed off and dissolved into dust, leaving the form of a young man in his late teens behind. He quickly looked around and left the rubble.

*   *   *

Adelaide peeked through a hole in the brick wall of the partially torn-down building and watched as Henry pried something out of his scaly clawed hand. Once he was back to his normal human form, he replaced the object around his neck. When he looked left and right, she quickly ducked down to make sure she wasn't noticed.

She had followed the dragon as best she could once the fight had taken place. Excited that his wing was torn and he couldn't fly away, she then felt guilty for delighting in her friend's suffering.

As Henry left the building, Adelaide continued following him. He moved quickly through the streets and alleys of the city, changing directions suddenly several times, which made it hard to predict when he was going to turn. Once he would turn, she found herself running to reach the opening before he could make another turn and disappear. Most of the streets still had people on them, so the sounds of her hurried footsteps were mostly drowned out by the passersby.

143

Adelaide followed Henry until they reached the edge of the city where abandoned buildings were being reclaimed by the wilderness. Here she had to be even more careful, as any noise she made would draw attention to herself. Most of the buildings had broken walls, twisted metal beams, and piles of brick and cement lying around. Vines, grasses, and trees grew out of the floors and climbed the crumbling walls.

One of these buildings was noticeably more overgrown than the others. She watched as Henry walked back and forth between large tree trunks and piles of rubble before disappearing near the farthest, darkest corner.

She snuck up to where she last saw him as quietly as possible. The idea that he was onto her and was just waiting to attack once she turned a corner made her heart race. Part of the roof or second floor of this building was still intact in this corner. Several large trees grew up toward the edge of the broken ceiling in such a way that they almost formed a living wall and created a dark, shadowed area. It wasn't until she stepped into the shadows and let her eyes adjust that she saw the steps leading down.

Adelaide cautiously made her way down the stairs, keeping one hand on the wall for support and guidance. She took her time with each step, gently testing the ground ahead of her, before shifting her weight forward. The farther down she went, the darker it got, and she had no desire to step into a pit or onto a sharp piece of metal.

When she reached the bottom of the steps, she slowly felt her way around the small room until she found a large hole in the wall. On the other side, there was a more natural passageway. Adelaide crept quietly into the tunnel, her heart pounding in her ears. Thoughts of Henry catching her or falling into an unseen pit gave her an adrenaline-heightened alertness.

Eventually, after many twists and turns, a soft blue-white light shone into the tunnel. Adelaide slowed her pace even more, fighting the urge to run ahead. When she reached the end of the tunnel, she gasped at what she saw.

The cavern before her contained a tranquil pond surrounded by trees. The trees were more twisted than seemed normal, with many branches that curved in odd directions and large roots that protruded from the stone floor. A gently shifting orb in the center of the cave near the top provided the area's light source. There were no signs of sunlight shafts or electrical equipment, so she wasn't sure what powered the orb or how trees could grow down here.

The faint sound of someone sighing caught her attention, and she saw Henry standing off to the right near one of the trees. He removed the object from around his neck and placed it in a crevice where two roots intersected.

And then his body slumped, just like the dragon's had.

Adelaide watched as the young man's body sloughed off and turned to dust, revealing a boy. He looked like he was only a couple years younger than her, but he was rather small and frail. She watched as the boy climbed across the roots and sat down near the water's edge. He seemed to stare for a moment at the dark depths before rocking his body back and forth slightly for a few minutes.

After a while, he looked up at the glowing orb. The orb burst into a million points of light, which began swirling above the lake, shifting through various shades of blue and green.

*   *   *

Henry sat at the edge of the lake and leaned back into a tree trunk. He was finally at peace in his home. In the world above, he was constantly on guard lest anyone realize he was as weak as he really was. Henry had always been a frail child, which made him vulnerable in the harsh world of the factories. The cavern was his refuge and home; a place where he could relax and not worry about being destroyed by those around him.

The fire-sprites swirled before him, and he stared adoringly at the various colors they produced. He reached out as some of them flew over and began to swirl around his hand and body. He felt peace and comfort wash over him. Closing his eyes, he listened to the slight rushing wind of their movements and the soft musical sounds they made.

He absentmindedly traced the cuts on his right palm where the stone had dug into his flesh. Transforming into a slightly older yet much stronger version of himself was fairly simple, but the dragon form required a deeper connection to his body.

A small noise caught his attention, and the fire-sprites instantly changed to reds and oranges as he looked toward the passage into the cavern. A cloud of the tiny living sparks flew toward the opening and stopped. He leaned forward but saw nothing in their light. Apparently, they also saw nothing and returned to their calmer blues and greens. They stayed near the entrance, as if guarding it.

Henry appreciated the kindness of the fire-sprites. For the longest time, they were his only friends. His body was too weak and frail to survive in the harsh world above, so he had stayed down here for several years, ever since one sprite had saved his life.

Thinking back on that day brought tears of sorrow and gladness. He missed his parents and the sprite, but he felt great love for the creature that had saved him as a young child.

Progress came with a price, and the price had been the

lives of his parents who died in a collapsed and burning building when a factory had exploded. They were too poor to afford better lodgings in a better location, so they had been forced to live across the street from some new experimental factory. Whatever they were working on failed one night, and fiery shards of metal and stone tore through the walls of their flat.

Henry barely survived, shielded by his parents' bodies. Being a naturally frail child already, Henry had been huddled for warmth between them when the explosion happened. As soon as the first explosion went off and the building shook, they flung their bodies on top of him. He didn't understand what was happening until everything stopped moving, even his parents. Sometime later he realized the pain in his heart was as physical as it was emotional. A piece of shrapnel had pierced his ribs.

He didn't know how long he sat crying before the strange creature scurried across the walls toward him. It was a scrawny creature with a body and tail about a foot long. Various colors rippled across its scaly body as it looked at him, its long, pointed ears pulled back from its face.

He watched the strange creature, as its colors were fascinating. The creature shimmered in the firelight. Despite his interest, Henry could feel his eyelids growing heavier. His whole body felt weak, and eventually he could no longer keep his eyes open.

What he never saw, but learned later, was that the sprite cut open its own chest and removed half its heart. The creature placed it inside of Henry's chest, where it fused with his own and helped rapidly heal his ribs and organs.

The sprite took him back to the cave and brought him food. Slowly, he grew to trust the creature, and eventually it became his new family.

Adelaide was distracted on the assembly line as she tried to decide what to do. She knew Henry's true form and where he lived, but she wasn't sure if she should say something, and, if she did, how she should do it.

Time passed and she mindlessly assembled her pieces as they moved past her. When the mid-shift siren blared, she made her way to the loading docks to sit with Henry.

This night, he sat farther from the edge, as it had started raining heavily. Sitting down beside him, she unwrapped her meal and began to eat.

"My mother loved the storms," she commented.

Henry looked at her quizzically.

"When it rained hard enough, it was like being transported to another world. The brick buildings around us disappeared." Adelaide smiled. "It also helped wash away some of the grime and dirt from the factories. For at least one morning, the air would smell clean and the streets were less filthy."

Henry nodded in understanding. "When I was little, the thunder scared me. My parents would let me sit between them so that I'd feel safe."

"I'm sorry. I don't mean to bring up painful memories," she apologized.

"It's OK."

They spent the rest of the break in silence, watching and listening to the storm as the cool, mist-laden wind gently grazed their faces.

Henry pushed the last crate into the truck and wiped the sweat from his forehead. He could see thin rays of light peaking over the roofs of the city's buildings. A smile crept across his face at the thought of getting to talk to Adelaide again on their way home after the end of the shift.

A few minutes later, the buzzer went off, and he made his way to the other side of the factory where everyone else was leaving. Adelaide was waiting as usual.

They chatted while he walked her home.

"I've almost saved up enough for the typewriter and the textbook," Adelaide commented. "If I can teach myself how to type and learn more math, perhaps I can get a job in one of the offices instead of at the factory."

Henry smiled; "I'm sure you'll figure it out in no time." He was happy for her but sad for himself, since he wasn't sure what he wanted to do. He liked her motivation, but it sometimes made him feel like he wasn't living up to his full potential.

She looked at him. "What do you want to do? You probably save everything you make."

"Well, I don't really spend any more than I need to," he replied slowly. Why would she think he saved everything he made? Most people in the factory spent the larger part of their wages on food and rent. "Wait, what do you mean?"

Adelaide seemed to pause as he looked at her. "Well..."

"I have expenses like everyone else."

"Yeah, but..."

"But what?"

Adelaide sighed, "I know. I know about the cave and the, um..." she lowered her voice, "dragon."

Henry's eyes went wide as he stared at her. She knew?! How could he have been so careless... No wonder she'd been nice to him. She probably wanted to steal the other half of the sprite's heart that he kept around his neck or take advantage of his weakness in some other way.

"How long have you known?"

"I saw you transform a couple months ago when the gargoyles first attacked. I was curious, so I followed you after the second attack, and I saw the cave."

Henry considered the timeline. "You didn't start talking to me until after the first attack. You spied on me this whole time? Were you planning on using me somehow?"

"I was just curious at first," Adelaide reasoned. "I mean, it's not every day that you see someone transform into a dragon. I wasn't trying to trick you or anything. I like being your friend."

"I... I'm not sure what to make of this. I guess I'll see you tomorrow." Henry turned and headed down the first alley he came to, trying to put distance between them. He was mad at himself for being followed, and he wasn't sure he could trust Adelaide anymore. In one way, he felt betrayed by her spying on him, but logically, she hadn't actually done anything to hurt him. If she was really going to take advantage of his weakness by stealing the heart or selling the fire-sprites, then surely she would have done it already.

Henry wandered the city for a couple hours, lost in thought, before returning to the cave.

"We might need to leave soon," he said to the fire-sprites as they swirled around him.

*   *   *

The next day, Henry avoided Adelaide as best as he could. As soon as his shift ended, he began to make his way back to the cave.

A hand grabbed his arm, and he whirled around to see

Adelaide.

"Wait," she said, panting slightly. "I—"

A crash and several screams interrupted her. Henry turned as he caught the familiar sound of metal claws scraping on stone.

He seized the stone around his neck and flew into the sky. Looking down, he could see the metal gargoyles breaking through windows and tearing the streets apart. Bodies were torn asunder, their limbs scattered in the creatures' wake.

Diving down, he attacked the first one he came across as it leaped out of a third-story window. He took out his frustration on the metal horrors, rushing in straight lines from one to the next as he smashed, tore, and crushed them. Only too late did he realize his carelessness as almost a dozen more of the monsters dove out of the clouds and slammed him through a wall.

Frantically, he twisted and turned, trying to break them faster than they could squeeze through the broken wall. Metal claws tore his wings and raked his flanks. Henry's blood began to turn the dust to mud, but he finally crushed the last one.

Carefully, he limped out of the broken building. He needed to make sure they were gone before he transformed and became even more vulnerable.

Everything seemed clear, so he turned down an alley, hoping to find shelter again before changing.

"No!" screamed a voice from behind him, followed by the sound of tearing flesh and gurgling blood.

He turned to see Adelaide between him and one of the gargoyles that had been stalking him down the alley. Her lower body lay on one side of the alley while her torso lay on the other.

Rage filled Henry's eyes and pain constricted his

throat. He leaped on the beast and opened his mouth to shout.

A torrent of fire poured out of him instead of sound. Within seconds, the metal head and torso of the gargoyle were a molten puddle beneath him.

Henry turned to Adelaide and pried the stone from his hand. He fell back into his young adult form and rushed to her side. Somehow she was still alive, but not for long. His mind searched frantically for a solution.

"I'm so sorry," he cried, uselessly clutching her shoulders. There were several punctures in her chest from the creature's claws when it tore her in half. Her eyes began to dim.

The sight of the blood brought back a memory, and he looked at the stone in his hand. If half of the sprite's heart had kept him alive, maybe it could do the same for her. He rammed the stone into her chest near her heart and willed it to work. Henry slumped back into the form of a sickly child and watched as the stone began to glow and knit itself into her heart.

Adelaide's eyes opened wide and she screamed in pain.

Half the heart could keep her alive, but it wasn't enough to shift her broken body into a whole one.

*   *   *

In that moment, all she knew was pain. Her fingers clutched at her missing half, desperate and horrified. She looked up to see Henry kneeling over her. She saw him reach into his chest and expose a glowing shard of stone similar to the one she'd seen around his neck.

Adelaide tried to protest, but he pushed her hands away as he pulled the glowing shard from him. He held it closer to her chest, and as he released it, the shard snapped into place between her ribs.

"Concentrate. I know you hurt, but you have to push past the pain and concentrate on making yourself whole. That's the only way it will work," she heard him say.

Adelaide closed her eyes and focused as best as she could. She focused on stopping the pain, and her mind pushed down in an effort to reform her legs. She felt nothing at first, but then a strange tingling warmth began to spread out from her heart.

The pain began to subside until eventually all she had left was a dull ache through her body, from her head down to her toes.

She opened her eyes to see her body restored.

Adelaide looked up at Henry with a smile. "Thank you," she began, before stopping abruptly as she saw his body begin to fade.

"Thank you for being my friend," he said with a smile moments before his body slumped and collapsed into dust.

Adelaide lurched forward, clawing at the pile of dust, but it was too late. Tears streamed down her face as her throat tightened. A second later, her whole body shuddered with her sobs.

*   *   *

Later that day, Adelaide made her way down the stairs and through the tunnels to Henry's home. She wasn't sure what she would say to the strange glowing things that had lived down there with Henry, but she was sure that they had been his friends. They needed to know what had happened.

Adelaide found the dark cavern and lit a match to see her way. Carefully shielding her light from the breeze near the tunnel, she searched inside, but no lights sprang forth in

153

response.

As she approached the trees that surrounded the pond, she noticed that all of their leaves had fallen. The tranquil pond had dried up noticeably, leaving a smaller pond surrounded by a larger area of stone floor. She moved closer and held up her match. The trees themselves looked old and withered.

Adelaide's hand dropped away from the tree nearest her, and the match slipped from her fingers. She didn't care that it bounced off a rock and landed in the water rather than becoming nestled between any of the bone-dry roots at her feet.

Darkness enveloped her. Adelaide stood there in the abyss for some time, not thinking about much of anything. After a while, she turned and stumbled out of the cave. The sun had started to set by the time she reached the surface.

Adelaide was filled with grief and fatigue. She had no interest in returning to the factory, and she was sick of the city that had robbed her of everyone she'd ever cared about. She didn't want to be around people, at least for a while.

Tripping over a root, her body lurched toward the ground. Her paws hit the packed dirt, preventing her face from doing the same. The world before her became clearer to see, and she continued on her way.

The large black cat slipped silently through the rubble of abandoned buildings and disappeared into the woods.

VIII

Journey Beyond
Dynoltir, +3052 TR

Three hundred seventy-eight years ago...

Five ships rocketed above the plane of Terra Prime's solar system, headed for a point somewhere above Helios, the star at the center. Six warships of the Colonial Alliance followed in close pursuit.

"Captain, the Alliance ships are demanding that we halt and prepare to be boarded," warned the communications officer on the bridge of one of the three Separatist warships trailing behind the two colony seed ships.

"Ignore them. Let me know as soon as they ready their weapons," Captain Seneca ordered. "Signal the gate guards and make sure that thing is ready."

"Aye, sir."

The atmosphere on the bridge was tense. The Alliance had discovered that they were planning to leave with technologies that had not been dutifully disclosed to their fellow colonies. This was seen as a threat that must be stopped, but they couldn't risk destroying what the Separatist ships carried. Most likely, they'd fire EMP missiles to knock out the Separatist warships before disabling the seed ships' engines. The Alliance could be more reckless with the Separatist warships than the seed ships. The five ships were traveling faster than drones could match.

"Sir, the gate guards report 'ready.' The gate is active and on standby. As soon as we make it through, the safety protocols will be activated."

A large round object took shape in the distance. The ships increased their speed.

155

"Sir, the Alliance is readying weapons!"

"Launch the defensive drones!"

Hundreds of small drones poured out of the five fleeing ships. The Alliance vessels each launched their own missiles. The drones swarmed to intercept and detonate the missiles prematurely.

The captain watched the monitor displaying the progress of the drones as they raced to cross the detonation threshold before the missiles.

No one breathed as the drones crossed the line and detonated the missiles only a few meters shy of their objective.

The collective sigh of relief was cut short as a plasma beam arced past the main display and struck the engines of one of the two seed ships.

"Order the seed ships to release all drones and signal the other two warships to turn around. We have to engage the enemy to allow them to escape."

Thousands of defensive, offensive, and exploratory drones streamed out of the seed ships as the three Separatist warships turned about and launched their own. Every Separatist laser and plasma weapon unleashed war onto the Alliance fleet.

The pursuing Alliance fleet was undaunted, crossing the safety threshold for using nukes. As they entered the cloud of drones, they launched their own. Their superior armor and size minimized the effect of the Separatist weapons.

"How close are the seed ships?"

"One hundred kilometers."

"If the Alliance pushes through, we won't be able to stop them." The captain paused. "Alert the other ships. We must protect the seeds."

The three Separatist warships flew into the Alliance

formation and detonated their self-destructs. The Alliance's ships were destroyed.

Moments later, the two seed ships entered the giant ring and disappeared. Engines ignited on the construct, and it began descending toward Helios. A handful of small ships that had been guarding it flew into its maw and also disappeared.

The giant construct broke apart and was destroyed in the atomic fires of Helios.

*   *   *

The present...

Captain Yana sat on the bridge of the Daedalus gazing out of the main display at the super gate before her. The Separatists had spent the last few centuries developing their technology and gathering resources in the safety of the galaxy's outer reaches. The culmination of their efforts now floated before her.

She looked down at her data pad and reviewed the details of the mission for the tenth time. The Daedalus, an inter-galactic seed ship, would travel through the super gate, and deploy the phase 2 pods. These contained the modular components of another super gate. The modular components of the gates were pre-programed to self-assemble once launched. A new unstable wormhole would be launched deeper into the new galaxy. They would send a drone and then relaunch the wormhole if the preliminary readouts were clear. At each stopping point in their journey, they would erect a new gate and recalibrate their star charts. Each stopping point would have two gates that would serve as a backup in an emergency. This pattern would continue until ten new sets of gates were created and the ship reached its final destination, a point in space where researchers were predicting the

157

possibility of a stable, naturally occurring wormhole.

The captain's chair was positioned in the center of the bridge with the pilot's station directly in front of it. Behind both stations and wrapping around the inside of the bridge were a series of consoles and workstations from which various engineering, scientific, or even defensive functions could be monitored and performed. At the moment, her second in command, Commander Tal, was greeting the rest of the crew and verifying their security clearances. For now, the only other crew member present was the pilot running through the pre-launch checklist.

Turning her attention to the pilot, she asked, "What is our status?"

"All modules are attached and checked. The final crew has just arrived... Huh?"

"What is it?"

"All the readouts just flickered," replied the pilot. "I'll run a systems check, but everything seems fine now."

"Let me know the results and meet us in the mess hall in 10 minutes for the mission briefing."

"Aye, ma'am."

*   *   *

Commander Tal stood in a corner of the mess hall that allowed him a clear line of sight on the entrance way. He watched as the crew entered and took their seats.

Professor Grimm sat down in the single row of chairs and leaned back. He was slightly past middle aged with hair that was already completely white. His head swiveled around the entire room as if examining every detail of his new environment. When he turned and faced Tal, he smiled and nodded. Tal's brow furrowed when he saw the professor's metallic blue eyes again. They had met many years previously, and it had taken a long time for Tal to not resent being stranded.

The professor's assistant, Miranda, was next. She sat next to her mentor, back straight, eyes aimed forward, and long dark hair pulled back into a ponytail. From Tal's research on the crew, he knew she was highly educated and disciplined, but not much else.

The ship's medical officer, doctor Kira Edwards, arrived a couple minutes later. She had a kind face and long red hair that she kept tied back. She sat down and began reading something on her data pad. Large-scale armed conflict was not common in the outer reaches of the galaxy, but conflict did occur and accidents did happen in space. The ship's medical officer had seen more severe injuries and conflict than most and had earned high regard for her skills.

Anthony Booth, the bureaucratic representative of High Command arrived next. His clean, perfectly pressed clothes were made of finer materials than were worn by any of the crew. Tal was sure he could even smell the man from where he sat. Booth was a representative of the legislative body that ultimately oversaw the Space Fleet High Command. Tal watched as the man took one of the chairs and moved it over to one side of the front of the room and sat with his back to the wall.

James Nix, the ship's engineer, walked in and quickly glanced around before taking his seat. From where he stood, Tal could see the man dutifully reviewing system specs on his data pad. His hair was short and his posture a bit stiff, but Tal knew from his file that this man was focused and practical.

The pilot, Cheng, arrived with Captain Yana. The pilot took the last seat farthest from the door as the captain took her place at the front of the room.

The captain stood with feet shoulder-width apart and her arms clasped behind her back. "I want to welcome all of you to this mission. We will be traveling through the super gate at 0800 tomorrow. The scouting probes all reported clear conditions. Once there, we will launch the first two self-assembling gates. It will take approximately 24 hours for the ship to scan and recalculate the star charts from our new position. During that time, the gates will be assembled and tested. From there, we will launch new scouting probes through the gate farther into the galaxy to examine the next stop on our journey. At each jump point, we will repeat the process of assembling the new gates and sending probes ahead to scout the next jump point after the ship recalculates the star charts."

"Why don't we just send an automated system to set up each of these jump points without a manned crew?" asked the medical officer.

The professor leaned forward to answer, but paused, looking at the captain. The captain nodded to him and he continued, "Since the new galaxy is tens of thousands of light years away, everything we know about the position of the stars and planets is tens of thousands of years out of date. At each jump point we will need to scan the visible arrangement of objects in all directions and recalculate the new star charts. Fully self-sufficient AI is outlawed, so any unexpected events missed by the probes could easily derail the mission without allowing us to know what happened. A manned crew can troubleshoot the situation better and relay any necessary intel, should an emergency arise."

"So, what's our final destination then, since we're remapping the galaxy at every jump point?" asked the pilot.

"Based on previous observations and a complex set of calculations, we have extrapolated where we think we may find naturally occurring wormholes. Even with the recalculated star charts, we are fairly confident of the location, as it is relative to other objects," answered Miranda.

"Thank you Professor Grimm and Dr. Everett. The final contingency that we need to review is the possibility of encountering extraterrestrial life. As you all know, Praxis shows no signs of sentient life other than humanity. We cannot discount the possibility, however unlikely, that this may not be true in Castor. The final aspect of our mission is to investigate any signs of sentient life and assess the potential threat to humanity. The safety of this crew supersedes any scientific discovery, but the safety of the human race supersedes all else. Does anyone have any questions or concerns?"

Tal watched as everyone either shook their head or looked around the room at the rest of the crew.

"With no further questions, you are dismissed. Be ready at your stations to depart at 0800 tomorrow," the captain concluded.

*   *   *

The next morning at 0800, Cheng found himself leaning forward slightly in excitement. He forced himself to relax and leaned back into the pilot's seat as he steered the ship toward the gate. This would be the first starship to enter an unexplored galaxy.

Unconsciously, he held his breathe as the ship entered the gate's swirling vortex. The usual lurch, as if his body suddenly sped up and slowed down, was slightly more drawn out this time. A new star field lie ahead of him, one he had never seen before.

"Captain, welcome to Castor," he said as he took in the sight of stars that no human had yet seen from this

161

perspective.

"Professor, deploy the first gate modules. Mr. Cheng, prepare to move into position for the next deployment," commanded Captain Yana.

"Primary gate modules launched. Assembly protocols initiated," replied Grimm.

"Moving to secondary deployment position," announced Cheng. He piloted the ship forward several hundred kilometers so that the two gates would be at a safe distance.

"Deploying the second set of modules and initiating self-assembly," said the professor.

"Thank you, gentlemen," replied the captain. "Mr. Cheng, initiate the star scans and chart updates."

"Yes, ma'am," he replied. Cheng reached over to the console on his left and activated the scanning sequence. "Scan initiated. We should be ready to proceed in about 24 hours."

"Thank you," finished the captain.

Cheng leaned back and watched the monitors displaying the new constellations. As the ship's pilot, he was used to having his back to the rest of the crew and ignoring most of their murmurings and conversations.

An alert sounded from one of his consoles, and he leaned forward to examine it more closely.

"Captain, we're picking up a signal from a nearby planet. It appears to be repeating itself every 23 seconds," he said.

"We didn't send any satellites or probes ahead of this ship, other than the one just before the jump, did we?" asked the professor.

"Negative," replied Yana. "What can you tell me about the planet?"

"From this distance, it appears to be an empty planet,"

remarked Miranda from her station.

"I suggest sending a contingent of probes to scout out the satellite and the planet before we approach," advised the professor.

"Agreed," replied Yana.

Cheng watched the cloud of scouting drones as they poured from the ship's sides and rocketed toward the nearby planet. This mission was turning out to be even more exciting than he had expected, possibly on the brink of first contact.

*   *   *

The seed ship lingered in the space between the two assembling gates like a large metallic whale. The central section of the ship's structure held a vast cargo bay containing the semicircular modules that would be separated and reassembled into the new gates.

On the rear end of the cargo bay were the ship's engines. A structural spine connected the command module all the way to the engines. Unlike an actual whale, there were auxiliary "spines" running along the sides of the ship. This provided alternative routes to the engines should an emergency arise.

At the front of the ship was the command module. This housed the bridge, quarters, labs, galley, and the ship's supply of drones. The command module also contained back-up engines and could be disengaged from the rest of the ship in an emergency.

While a complex computer system existed within the ship to enable control and monitoring of all systems, there was no autonomous AI capable of controlling it. With few exceptions, all information was recorded by the ship's various sensors and would sit in waiting until one of the authorized

163

human occupants accessed it. Exceptions existed for algorithms that routinely monitored for maintenance and life support faults. High Command had learned centuries ago not to trust AI completely.

Due to the unknown circumstances awaiting the mission in a new galaxy, the ship had been equipped with an elaborate 3-D printing lab. Not only was it able to print replacement parts and tools, it could even construct and assemble the requested items into moving and functioning devices.

While the gates finished assembling and activating, the ship's command crew began to move the ship toward the source of the unknown signal.

As the ship began to move, the cameras in and near the 3-D construction lab shut off, and its doors locked. Inside the room, the consoles came to life, displaying a series of schematics in quick succession. After a moment for calibration, the printers began to move.

*   *   *

Thousands of probes punched through the alien world's thin atmosphere, deactivating their shields as they approached the surface. They quickly spread out in all directions, scanning and mapping the planet's surface as they flew.

The drones soared over the flat plains, dipped in and out of gorges, and rose over the mountains. As they went, small detectors opened up to take air samples for analysis. Tiny cameras and microphones recorded every sight and sound. Precise measurements were taken by way of lasers sent out from the drones to calculate distances, heights, and depths. A few drones even landed to collect soil samples as well.

It would take the drones several hours to complete

their preliminary planet scan. Most flew high, some landed, and a very few found their way into an underground cave system.

*   *   *

The professor eagerly watched the data coming in from the probes. Most of the drones were already mapping the planet, while some had taken positions around the alien satellite in order to observe it. He was so fascinated by the new discoveries that he hadn't been able to decide which to focus on, so now he sat slightly farther from the station than normal and watched both sets of data simultaneously.

The planet's features were so far barren of any signs of life. A landscape of rocks, mountains, valleys, and plains was slowly being constructed on the screen in front of him.

The satellite was roughly cylindrical, made of what appeared to be a chemically treated metal so that it had a deep red color. A few rectangular panels were detected by very slight seams. Dotted around the satellite were disks with a series of holes around the perimeter of each disk.

"Professor, I repeat, what is the status of the gates?" interrupted the captain's voice.

Shaking himself back to the world around him, he spun in his chair to face her. "They are assembled and both have connected successfully back to Praxis."

"Thank you, professor," she replied. "Since you find your probes so much more fascinating, what have they discovered?"

Vaguely aware of Yana's subtly scolding tone, Grimm smiled; "The planet shows no signs of life so far. The satellite has no discernible defenses and has continued to broadcast the same signal, repeating approximately every twenty-three

165

seconds."

"Do we know what it means yet?"

"The sample is quite short, and we have no external reference points from which to start, unfortunately. Perhaps, we should take a closer look? I mean, since all signs indicate that the device is non-hostile and no threats have yet been detected on the planet..."

The captain paused before issuing the order, "Mr. Cheng, proceed to the planet. Professor, prepare the examination bay."

"Yes, ma'am!" he said as he shot out of his seat and headed to the door. As he moved, he saw Miranda begin to follow him and felt the ship lurch slightly as it headed to investigate the satellite and the planet.

"Steady, Mr. Cheng, this may be a momentous event, but steady minds are more useful than excited ones," admonished the captain.

*   *   *

Yana stood in the observation room waiting for the professor and Miranda to finish suiting up in the airlock to her left. Directly in front of her was a large window that allowed her to see the quarantine bay and its new contents: the alien satellite.

"Make sure to attach your tethers as soon as you enter the bay. I will not hesitate to jettison the artifact if it threatens the ship in any way," said Commander Tal from her right. He released the comm button and brought his hand closer to the controls in front of him.

She turned back toward the bay as the two scientists entered. Tal was harsh, but right.

The device in front of her was essentially a large

166

cylinder on its side. It was approximately 3 meters long and 2 meters in diameter. Metal plates comprised the device's outer shell, though most of the seams were nearly imperceptible. In addition, there were signs that micro meteors had scratched and dented the device, implying it had been in position for quite some time.

Her thoughts had turned to the strange markings on the metal when Grimm began narrating his investigation.

"Preliminary examinations only show one possible hatch on the device," reported the professor as he walked around the satellite and stopped before a section marked out by a large rectangular seam. In the center of this panel was a disk with six holes around its outer edge.

Grimm took a clamp and locked its prongs into the holes on either side. He then began to turn the disk. As it rotated, sliding bolt sounds could be heard inside the device. The disk stopped and the metal plate began to slide out of position, coming completely loose all at once and plummeting toward the floor.

Miranda's body dropped in her stance and her hands shot forward to catch the plate. The captain was impressed. The assistant was stronger than she appeared.

"Thank you, Miranda," said Grimm with what sounded like a smile.

"You're welcome," came the stoic reply.

Miranda set the plate carefully to the side, and they both turned back toward the inner workings of the device. On the far left was what appeared to be a digital display. Just to its right was another panel that contained an array of buttons, each marked with an unusual symbol. Beyond that were the exposed components of the satellite.

After several moments of visual examination, the professor turned to the panel of buttons.

"Let's see what this does," he said and pressed one. The device emitted a strange, high-pitched sound, and the ship's lights blinked. A circular aperture opened up inside the device, emitting a red holographic image of a planet. Grimm stepped back and Miranda froze. More symbols from the alien language appeared next to the planet, and the whole image began to pulse.

"The signal stopped and it's scanning the ship," said Miranda as she looked up from her data pad.

"Don't!" the professor said, turning to the observation window and extending his palm out toward Tal. "It's translating," he pointed to the projection as the symbols began changing rapidly, sometimes flickering into the human alphabet.

Yana also raised her hand, palm flat and facing out as a sign to Tal to hold off on ejecting the satellite. She could see his brow furrow from the corner of her eye.

"Please proceed with caution," she said, pressing the comm button on the wall to her left.

The professor nodded and turned back to the device. A series of strange symbols began scrolling across the screen.

"It's stopped scanning the ship," informed Miranda.

"Fascinating," said the professor, looking at the projection. "It's the planet below us."

The alien symbols were gone. In their place were letters Yana could understand, though only some of the words made sense.

DANGER!!! QUARANTINE!!! HATCHLING!!!

The captain spun and hit the comm button on the wall; "Recall the drones now!"

*   *   *

Deep under the planet's surface, a group of approximately one hundred drones flew through a series of twisting tunnels. The materials of the planet's crust were such that no signals from the seed ship reached them. Without new directives, they continued on their original mission.

Eventually the tunnels opened up into a vast cavern. The drones scanned the upper surface and walls, mapping this new expanse. Below the ceiling of jagged rocks was a surface dissimilar from that of the preceding tunnels.

The material seemed to undulate slightly, but when the drones approached to acquire a sample, they discovered that it was not a liquid. They proceeded to land and attempted to gather scrapings, but the material, despite being flexible enough to ripple across the cave floor, was too hard to extract.

Several of the drones formed a circle on the strange material and began cutting into it with their lasers. The floor twitched and shuddered.

Then it lurched upward, smashing the drones into the cave ceiling.

*   *   *

Grimm stared at the monitor in the lab as the alien code scrolled past. He didn't know if the symbols represented sounds or entire concepts, but he looked for patterns in their arrangement and sequencing to grasp their secrets.

"I've completed my review of the drones' data," interrupted Miranda.

His head snapped up; "Oh, anything interesting? Did they find life?"

"No. The mappings show no bodies of water, and none of the samples show signs of life. The only oddity is that one hundred of the drones are unaccounted for. Their last

transmissions show them entering a cave system, but nothing
else after that.”

“We need to know what happened to them. Prepare
another set and program them to take positions along the
underground paths so that they can form a signal chain. If
there's anything down there to find, it's probably in those
caves.”

*   *   *

The captain sat in her quarters, her eyes closed. Her
door was locked, so she was finally separated from everyone
else. Her mind relaxed as she let go of the stern demeanor she
wore when dealing with the crew. Until the warning of the
satellite was resolved, she could not relax fully, but for now,
she could take a brief rest. The weight of responsibility and
professionalism dropped from her, and she put on a pair of
headphones and laid back on her bed. Her mind floated with
the music, her imagination conjuring images and stories
inspired by the lyrics and the feelings evoked by the sounds.

Slowly her consciousness began to drift off into
darkness.

A loud beep shocked her back awake and she yanked
the headphones off. She pushed the comm button on the wall
next to her bed; “Report.”

“Captain, the planet is breaking apart,” came the pilot's
voice.

Grogginess slowed her faculties; “What?”

“The planet's crust is breaking apart. I've moved the
ship back a safe distance, but this might be what the satellite
was referencing.”

The captain could feel her mind redressing itself in the
weighty clothes of her position.

170

"I'm on my way. Wake the rest of the crew and sound the alarm."

*   *   *

Grimm rushed onto the bridge and stared at what lay beyond; "Amazing..."

This must have been what the alien message meant by "hatchling." The monster being born in front of him was fascinating to behold.

The shattered remains of the planet's crust slowly peeled away from the surface of the creature. Its main body was amorphous with thousands of relatively thin tendrils reaching out in all directions. Grimm watched as the tendrils interacted with the remnants of the planet's crust. After blindly groping about, they began to curl around the largest chunks of rock.

The creature rotated to reveal a ring of twenty large tentacles, each roughly the same length as its body's diameter. These tentacles quickly crushed and pulled the larger chunks of rock into its maw.

"Professor, activate the primary gate and send everything we're currently recording back to Praxis. Mr. Cheng, maintain our distance. I don't want this creature getting any closer than it already is," commanded the captain.

Grimm turned around and activated the primary gate's remote control, dialing it back to their home galaxy. He confirmed that the gate activated through his view on the monitor.

"Connection is achieved, and we are transmitting," he informed the captain.

"Hey, do you see this?" asked Cheng.

Grimm turned back around to see that the creature's

171

tendrils had started twitching and pointing in the direction of the gates.

"Fascinating. It appears the tendrils can detect disturbances in space-time," he mused.

A moment later, the creature's body deformed into a more oblong shape with its tentacles forming a spear point on one end. An intense green plasma began to form around the creature, and it rocketed past them toward the gate.

"Shut it down!" commanded Yana and Tal simultaneously.

Grimm hurriedly disabled the gate; "Done."

The creature slowed and began reaching out in all directions again as if lost and exploring its surroundings.

*　　*　　*

"We should find a way to destroy it," muttered Tal grumpily from the back of the room.

"We can't do that; this is the greatest scientific discovery of our time. It's the first alien life we've ever encountered. It could be the last of its species!" implored Grimm.

"We can't use the gates without attracting its attention," observed Cheng.

"If we return to Praxis via a gate, we run the risk of bringing it back to Praxis and endangering the rest of humanity," argued Tal.

"We can't return; we have a mission to complete within the deadline," warned Booth.

"The safety of humanity and this crew takes precedence," admonished the captain.

"I'm not suggesting that we take unnecessary risks, only that we can't afford delays—"

172

"While I appreciate scientific discovery, human lives are more important than some wormhole," interrupted Yana.

"Unless there's some other reason, this mission is time sensitive," questioned Tal.

"No, there's nothing else," said Booth as he sat back down.

"In that case, the most prudent course of action is to return to Praxis, gather more offensive resources, and return later to deal with the creature." Yana pondered for a moment. "We'll position ourselves as close to the gate as possible in a position that is farthest from the creature and activate the gate just before entering it."

*   *   *

Yana and the crew returned to the bridge. She did not like having to abort the mission so early, but the safety of her crew took priority.

"Mr. Cheng, move us into position," she ordered.

"Turning about and heading to the gate," confirmed Cheng.

Yana turned to the scientist; "Grimm, prepare to activate the gate on my command."

"Ready," he reported.

The ship began to turn so that it could head back to the gate. The creature's small tendrils on the main monitor began to twitch. As the ship picked up speed, their movements became more erratic.

"Professor?"

"I see it," he responded.

A moment later, the creature's plasma shell began to reform.

"I think it senses the ship's engines."

"Cheng, increase speed and take evasive action. Don't let that thing catch us."

"On it."

The ship's speed increased, and the creature took chase.

"Cheng, take us away from the gates as far as possible. Professor, activate the positioning jets on the gates and have them move farther apart. We're going to use one as bait and detonate it before the creature reaches it."

"On it," came the simultaneous replies.

The ship raced away from the gates as the two gates began moving farther apart.

"Turn the ship around and aim for the farthest gate, but make sure we pass close the nearest one first. As soon as we pass the gate, activate it. When the creature changes targets, detonate the gate."

Cheng steered the ship around in a long arc so as to avoid the creature changing trajectory to get to them sooner. Once the ship was lined up, they raced toward the gates, the creature following close behind and slowly gaining.

"Now," commanded Yana as they passed the first gate.

The professor sent the signal, and the gate activated. For a brief moment, the creature slowed down as if sensing the greater energy of the gate.

As soon as it shifted direction, Yana gave the order; "Detonate."

The gate exploded in a brilliant flash. The creature's tentacles and tendrils writhed in confusion.

"Take us through the remaining gate," she commanded.

"Activated," reported the professor as the swirl of energy appeared in the giant ring.

*   *   *

The ship rocketed through the gate, and the universe disappeared in a brilliant flash of light. A moment later they dropped back into reality, and the stars came into view.

All was calm for a moment until the captain and crew realized that none of the constellations looked right, and there were no space stations. The space around them was empty.

"Where are we?" asked the captain. "This isn't the launch point in Praxis."

"We're further into the galaxy. Activating the scans to re-map the stars," replied Cheng.

"How did this happen?"

"A signal was sent to the gate just before we entered. It changed the destination," informed Tal.

*   *   *

The captain burst into Booth's quarters.

"I know you were the one who gave the command to the gate. Do not defy my orders again, or I will have you thrown out an airlock. I cannot have anyone unnecessarily jeopardizing the safety of this crew."

"You can threaten me all you like, captain," he said as he sat down calmly behind his desk. "You and I both know that you only command this ship at the leisure of High Command. I am here as the ultimate representative of the High Command. If I give the order, you will no longer be in command of this ship."

"We are a long way from High Command, Booth. Anything can happen in the outer reaches. If you're in such a hurry and willing to risk all our lives on a blind jump, then it must be something truly important that we're after. What is

175

it?"

"This isn't a scientific expedition, it's a preemptive military mission. The satellite that the professor's been fawning over isn't the first evidence of sentient life. High Command recently discovered an artifact in Praxis that spoke of a weapon of untold power. That is what we're after, and now that we have confirmation that there are other sentient creatures in this galaxy, we can't waste any time or risk the weapon falling into enemy hands. No cost is too high for the safety of the entire human race."

Appendix I

Space and Time

Each tale in The Wanderer's Notebook references a place and a time. These places are part of a collection of ten worlds, or universes, that are connected via the same world tree. Travelers hoping to escape their universe to see what lies beyond are only able to travel to one of the other nine worlds that have blossomed from that tree.

The tree itself sits in a vast garden of similar trees, all with varying numbers of worlds nestled in their branches. Niwltir, Dynoltir, and Faetir are just three of the ten worlds that blossomed in tree number 3,891.

Niwltir's most notable characteristic is the timeless mists that separate the various lands contained within. Within the mists themselves, there is no time or space, and most who enter never return. If someone spends enough time near the land's mist wall boundary, the mist will slowly recede to reveal new terrain and vegetation that did not previously exist.

Faetir is a world with a malleable reality. This is how the sprites and other inhabitants can manipulate their surroundings at will and avoid permanent consequences to their actions.

Dynoltir is the world of humans, most similar to your own world. One of the more notable exceptions is that the home planet of humanity in Dynoltir, Terra Prime, has only one massive continent. Because of this, some historic events may be similar to the ones with which you are familiar, while others may be completely different.

The dating system referenced at the beginning of each tale is unique to each world. Dynoltir uses TR, or Terran Reckoning. This roughly approximates your AD/BC dating

177

system. Due to the malleability of reality in Faetir, time has little meaning there. Until or unless they visit one of the other worlds, the inhabitants tend to not grasp the concept of time. Tales taking place in Niwltir tend to use ER, otherwise known as Elvish Reckoning.